EVERYTHING
CHANGES

Visit us at www.boldstrokesbooks.com

EVERYTHING CHANGES

by

Samantha Hale

2014

EVERYTHING CHANGES

ISBN 13: 978-1-62639-303-5

This Trade Paperback Original Is Published By
Bold Strokes Books, Inc.
P.O. Box 249
Valley Falls, NY 12185

First Edition: September 2014

CREDITS
EDITORS: LYNDA SANDOVAL AND CINDY CRESAP
PRODUCTION DESIGN: SUSAN RAMUNDO
COVER DESIGN BY SHERI (GRAPHICARTIST2020@HOTMAIL.COM)

Acknowledgments

Many thanks to Helen, for making me not just a better writer, but a better person. To Angele, for being a sounding board, a confidante, and a friend. And to Lisa & Nate, for your continued support and encouragement. This novel would never have been written if not for you.

CHAPTER ONE

There are two kinds of truth. There is the truth we tell so, technically, we are not lying, and there is the deeper, fuller truth. Raven was telling the truth when she told her friends she wasn't interested in any of the guys at school. That she had known most of them for far too long and too well to think of them in a romantic sense. Some of them she'd known since kindergarten and had seen through gapped teeth, knobby knees, braces, and voice changes. It was hard to think about kissing a guy you'd witnessed eat paste on a dare in third grade, or throw up his lunch at the fair in sixth.

The deeper, fuller truth was, Raven wasn't interested in any guys. She didn't watch movies and wait for the lead actor to take his shirt off. She didn't whistle at guys on the street like Summer did, or notice that the guy at the coffee shop who'd smiled at her was cute, like Chloe did.

She was seventeen years old and had never had a serious boyfriend. She'd never even really kissed a guy. There had been a few dates—one or two that ended in a good night kiss, but nothing more than a quick peck.

It was something she tried not to think about, too afraid of the implications to examine her feelings more closely. For the most part, she was able to shove it aside. But it was hard sometimes, when it seemed like all around her were happy couples and constant reminders that she didn't feel the same way about guys as her friends did. Chloe and AJ had been together for almost two years now, and it was clear from the way her face lit up when she talked about him that she was completely into him, and Summer was such a flirt, she hadn't been with anybody steady for a while now, though she'd had a few boyfriends.

It didn't help though, with Valentine's Day coming up, all she'd heard about for the past week and a half was everyone's romantic plans, and it once again brought everything to the surface.

"I hate Valentine's Day," Raven announced at lunch that day as she tossed her backpack onto the floor and took the empty seat across from Chloe and Summer.

"Problem, Rae?" Chloe asked, raising an eyebrow.

"Damn right I have a problem. Valentine's Day. I swear if I see one more stupid paper heart or cupid cardboard cutout…" She let out a frustrated sigh. She'd just come from a student council meeting, of which she was a member, and all everyone could talk about was the upcoming occasion. And what they should do for it. One person suggested candy-grams. Another roses. Raven had made an excuse and bailed before they could even start talking about the dance.

"Why don't you just ask someone out?" Chloe suggested. "I heard Derek is single again. Didn't he have a thing for you last year?"

"Derek?" Raven shrugged. Derek Nast was in their grade. She supposed he was cute. He was tall and lanky, with wavy brown hair that fell down into his eyes and a quick, easy smile.

He was a nice guy. They'd worked together on a history project last year and gotten along well.

She wasn't really interested in going out with him though. Especially not with the on-again, off-again relationship he seemed to have going with Chelsea Hanes. They'd broken up and gotten together a half dozen times since the beginning of the year.

"I don't want to date a guy just so I'll have someone to take me out for Valentine's Day."

"Julia's having a dinner party that night. A couple of her single friends from school," Summer said. "Want to crash it with me?"

Julia was Summer's older sister. She was two years older than them and a freshman in college. Summer, Chloe, and Raven had grown up tagging along after her. Over the years, they had gone from being annoying tagalongs to friends.

Julia had stayed close; her school was less than an hour away, and she came home often, bringing friends with her most of the time. Raven had spent enough time hanging around them at the house that it wouldn't be awkward or weird for her to join them for the evening.

"Is your mom cooking?" Raven asked. Mrs. Mitchell was an amazing cook. She had been a chef before leaving work to have kids.

"Probably. She'll help at least. Julia's okay, but Mom's cooking…"

Raven nodded. She knew.

"Sold."

"Great. I'll call you later with the details."

"Thanks, Summer," Raven said, feeling a little better now.

CHAPTER TWO

Having Julia's party to look forward to made the rest of the week bearable. Raven found she wasn't quite so annoyed by all the pink and red paper hearts plastered over nearly every available flat surface at the school or the overly sappy commercials for diamond rings and gold necklaces that played repeatedly on TV each night.

She was even starting to look forward to Valentine's Day. Going to a dinner party with friends wasn't quite the same as having someone to be with, but she decided to make the most of it. Especially considering it would probably be her last social outing for a while. Midterms were the following week, and when Raven's parents saw her marks, she would be grounded for the foreseeable future.

It wouldn't matter to them that the failing grade was in art. Her parents were both firm believers in a well-rounded education. And both of them had excelled in the arts. Her mom had been a dancer, and her father had busked his way through college. Nor would it matter that the rest of her grades were good. Even though it was only one class tripping her up, it would be enough to put her into the proverbial doghouse for a long while, so Raven was going to make the most out of what was likely to be her last weekend of freedom.

With that in mind, she found herself getting into the spirit of the holiday a little. On Friday before classes started, she bought a couple of the chocolate candy-grams that the student council was selling and sent them to Summer, Chloe, and AJ, cheesy message and all.

And on the way over to Summer and Julia's for dinner, she stopped at the corner store and picked up a flower for Julia, as a thank-you for letting her crash her dinner party. She wanted to get a rose, but those were ridiculously expensive this time of year so she got a carnation instead. It was pink and smelled sweet, so she figured that was good enough.

Summer had said dinner was at seven thirty, so Raven showed up around quarter to and let herself in the side door. She had been letting herself into and out of this house for so long now that she really didn't even give it a second thought. She and Summer had been friends since the first day of kindergarten, when they'd literally run into each other on the playground. They'd spent the rest of the day in the nurse's office together holding ice packs to their injuries and had been inseparable ever since. Even if Raven's nose still had a bump in it from being broken and Summer had a small scar on her bottom lip from where she'd bitten it almost completely through on impact. The Lewis household was just as familiar and comfortable to her as her own.

As she hung up her coat and kicked off her boots in the mudroom, she could hear the murmur of conversation coming from the kitchen, so after shedding her winter wear she headed down the hallway toward the sounds. She found Summer and Julia in there along with a mess of pots, pans, plates, and an array of silverware strewn across the counter.

"Looks more like a science experiment than a meal," she commented, taking note of the various bowls of seasonings and spices on the table and the measuring cups alongside them. "Smells kind of like it, too."

She was joking about that. Whatever Julia was cooking, it smelled amazing. Two seconds in the room and already Raven's mouth was watering.

Julia rolled her eyes and went back to stirring whatever was boiling in the pot on the stove.

"I got you something."

Julia glanced warily over her shoulder, and Raven held up the flower she'd purchased at the corner store.

"Aww, Raven, how sweet." She mimed wiping a tear from her eye.

"Well, if you don't want it…" Raven made a move to take it back, but Julia grabbed the stem from her hand.

"Never said that. Thanks, Rae. It's very pretty." Julia gave her a one-armed hug and sniffed deeply. "Smells nice, too."

"Geez, Jules. You're all covered in food stuff." Raven squirmed out of Julia's grip and examined her outfit, checking to make sure none of the sauce that had spilled down Julia's apron had gotten onto her clothes. She hadn't exactly gotten all dressed up or anything, just a pair of black jeans and a deep purple blouse, but still, she didn't want to spend the rest of the evening with dinner all down her side.

"Relax. You're fine."

It was Raven's turn to roll her eyes as she pulled out one of the kitchen chairs and slid onto it.

"So, what are you making?"

"Salad, spicy ravioli stuffed with ricotta cheese, garlic bread, and for dessert, chocolate mousse."

"Mom made the noodles this morning," Summer supplied. "And Jules has been perfecting her sauce for days now. It's amazing."

"I can't wait," Raven said. She had barely eaten anything all day in anticipation of tonight's meal. "Need a taste tester?"

"Nope. You've got to wait and taste it along with everybody else."

Raven had figured as much, but it had been worth a shot. "Speaking of, who else is coming tonight?"

"Cindy, Olivia, and Morgan."

Two out of the three, Raven knew. Cindy was one of Julia's roommates, and Olivia was a friend from her program. Raven had met them both on several occasions and liked them both. Morgan, Raven had never met but had heard mentioned a few times.

"They should be here any minute. Do you guys mind getting the table set up?"

"Mind, yes," Summer said. "But will we? Of course."

"And don't break anything, okay? Mom will kill me."

"In that case…" Summer gave her sister a devious smile as she stood and tugged Raven up out of her chair. The two of them exited into the dining room to the sounds of Julia muttering something about wishing she were an only child.

CHAPTER THREE

"Hey, Raven. There you are," Summer called out as she strode into the living room. As if she had not just left her sorting silverware in the dining room a few minutes ago. Raven rolled her eyes and ignored her, offering a wave and a "hey" to the room in general, as she took a seat on the couch next to the only unfamiliar face.

"So, I'm going to take a wild guess and say, you must be Raven," Morgan said, half turning in her seat to face Raven as she spoke.

"Uh…yeah. That's me." Raven found herself slightly tongue-tied in facing probably the prettiest girl she had ever seen.

"I'm Morgan."

Raven simply nodded.

Her reactions were a bit slow as she raised her arm to shake the proffered hand, but she managed to wrap her fingers around Morgan's and give a solid squeeze. She shivered slightly as callused fingertips slid against her skin as Morgan pulled away.

"Nice to meet you," she murmured belatedly, wincing slightly at the way her voice cracked a little on the last word. She licked her lips and cleared her throat as she tried to think of something else to say.

"You too." Morgan shifted, settling herself more comfortably on the couch, drawing one knee up beneath her as she draped an arm along the back of the couch. "So, what brings you to our little lonely hearts dinner?"

"Julia's cooking," Raven said with a shrug. "What about you?" She found it hard to believe that a pretty girl like Morgan wouldn't have received some offers.

"My girlfriend and I broke up just before school started. It was pretty rough. I'm just not ready to start dating again."

Raven's breath caught in her throat at Morgan's words.

"Wait, you're gay?" The question was out before she could censor herself, and she clapped a hand over her mouth in horror before anything else could spill out unintended.

Beside her, Morgan stiffened, the hand resting along the top of the couch tensed into a fist, the muscles in her cheek jumped as she clenched her jaw.

"Oh my God, I'm so sorry," Raven mumbled around her fingers, before slowly letting her hands fall into her lap. "That was rude. I'm sorry." She ignored the buzzing in her head and the way her pulse picked up at the news, and focused on her apology. "I'm not usually such a spaz. Please, just forget I even said that."

Beside her, Morgan relaxed, sagging back against the arm of the couch with a nod. Raven offered a smile and was pleased to see Morgan offer an answering one. "What I meant to say was, I'm sorry to hear that."

"Thank you," Morgan murmured softly. "But I'd really rather not talk about it, if you don't mind."

"Sure. Yeah. I get that." Raven nodded and then fell silent. She wracked her brain for something else to say, some other topic of conversation to guide them away from the awkwardness that now hung in the air between them. But it was hard to think of anything aside from the fact that the girl sitting next to her was gay. Morgan's hand, the one that rested on the back of the couch just inches from her shoulder, with its callused fingertips and clear-polished nails, held hands with other girls. And her eyes kept drifting to Morgan's lips. She couldn't help but wonder if it felt different, kissing girls.

Her musings were cut short just then, as Julia came in to announce that dinner was ready. The wonderful smells from the kitchen had started drifting into the living room so nobody had to be told twice to get moving, and within moments, they were seated around the dining room table, passing serving plates back and forth and handing around the condiments. The next few minutes were mostly silent as everyone sampled their food, which was delicious. The homemade vinaigrette on the salad was the perfect mix of sweet and spicy, the ravioli practically melted in your mouth, the noodles were so soft and tender, and the sauce was, as Summer promised, amazing.

"Wow, Jules. You really should think about following your mom into a career as a chef," Olivia said after her first few bites. The rest of the table murmured their agreement.

"I think you've just ruined all other food for me," Morgan added. "I don't know how I'm going to go back to eating cafeteria food now."

"How come you never cook like this at school?" Cindy asked. "The last time you made dinner it was macaroni and cheese. From a box. You know that's not going to fly anymore, right?"

Julia just laughed. "You do know we couldn't afford to eat like this every night, right?"

"I don't care. I'll be poor if it means I get to eat like this all year."

Raven let the conversation swirl around her, unable to focus or follow what the others were talking about. If anyone noticed that she was unusually silent throughout dinner, nobody commented on it.

It was Summer who pulled her out of her reverie as Julia cleaned up the dinner plates in preparation for dessert. Raven caught the end of her question, something about a last meal, and her brain scrambled to catch up, to figure out what Summer was talking about so nobody would notice she hadn't been paying attention.

"What do you mean, last meal?" Olivia asked, inadvertently clueing Raven into what Summer had said. A memory of a conversation at lunch the day before sprung into her head.

"Midterms are next week," Raven began her explanation. "And when I fail one of mine, my parents are going to kill me. I'm a dead man walking, and this is my last meal. And it was amazing." She raised her voice for the last part so Julia would hear her in the kitchen.

"You really think you're going to fail your exams?" Olivia asked.

"Just one of them. Art history. But it'll be enough to piss my parents off."

"Well, you know, I'm an art major," Morgan said. "If you want, I could help you cram over the weekend."

Raven glanced over at the girl she'd met only a few hours ago who had just offered to give up some of her weekend to help her study. The same one she'd been silently scrutinizing all night. Guilt warred with relief. "You would do that?"

"Sure. Beats the nothing I had planned."

Raven couldn't help but laugh at that. "Whatever. I'll take it."

Chapter Four

An hour later, they'd finished with dessert and had moved into the living room for a couple of decidedly unromantic movies. Julia had downloaded an assortment of action and horror flicks, anything she could find where someone or something got blown up.

Raven found herself squeezed in between Summer and Morgan on the couch, and the forced shoulder to hip contact was making her restless. The entire left side of her body was warm and tingly from the heat of Morgan so close to her. Morgan's hand rested against the side of her leg, and Raven was struck with the thought that it would be effortless to reach over and take it. She shook her head, trying to dispel the idea.

She tried to shift away, creating some space between them, but that had her leaning into Summer, who squirmed and wiggled against her weight, until finally elbowing her in the side to get her to move. Reluctantly, Raven eased into her original position, bringing her shoulder back to brushing up against Morgan's. A tremor ran down her arm at the contact.

She tried to ignore it and focused on the screen in front of her, but she couldn't quite get the nearness of Morgan out of her head. With that awareness came the memory of her earlier musings, of what it would be like to kiss a girl. She imagined it would be soft. Morgan's lips looked soft. Soft and shimmery. They'd probably taste like vanilla, or maybe cherry. She licked her own lips at the thought, imagining the feeling of Morgan's lips ghosting against her own, soft and supple and—she jerked in place, her entire body flushed and buzzing.

"Stop fidgeting," Summer said, jabbing her once again with her elbow.

"Sorry."

"What is with you?"

"Can't get comfortable."

"You okay?" Morgan's voice in her ear startled her, and the hand on her knee made her jump. She was on her feet without conscious thought of doing so and felt a blush heat her cheeks as she realized all eyes were on her.

"I have to pee," she announced.

"Yeah, thanks for sharing," Julia muttered, shaking her head.

Still blushing, Raven retreated from the room and escaped down the hall to the bathroom. She shut and locked the door behind her then leaned heavily against it, trying to calm her racing heart.

"What the hell was that?" she whispered, closing her eyes and taking a deep, steadying breath. Had she really just imagined kissing Morgan?

She shook her head, trying to clear it, but the images remained.

It doesn't mean anything, she told herself. She repeated the phrase over and over again, until her breathing had calmed and her heart rate had slowed.

Raven returned to the living room and settled on the floor in front of the couch, using it as a backrest and a shield from Summer's quizzical glances and the close contact bumping of knees and shoulders as she tried to concentrate on the movie playing across the TV screen. But the movie was already halfway through, and she just couldn't seem to catch up on it.

❖

"That was fun," Summer said as she pushed open the door of her room and strode across it to flop down onto her bed. "I'm glad you came."

"Yeah, me too," Raven agreed. She'd had a good time, despite some of the weirdness of the evening. "We need to find another occasion for Julia to cook, soon," she added, dropping into the beanbag chair in the corner.

"What's the next holiday? Easter?" Summer murmured.

"No, St. Patrick's Day's next month—think we could talk her into making us a meal?"

"Since when are you Irish?"

"It's St. Patty's day; everyone's Irish."

"Yeah, I want to watch when you try and sell that one to Jules."

Summer made a noncommittal humming noise and rolled onto her side to face Raven. "I'm going to miss you when your parents lock you away in your room." Though her words were teasing, there was a hint of seriousness in her voice.

"Maybe it won't happen. Maybe studying with Morgan this weekend will help."

"Hey, yeah, maybe," Summer said, her expression brightening at the prospect. "It was cool of her to offer to help you study."

Raven nodded. It really was. Morgan didn't have to offer up part of her weekend to help Raven out, but she had. "She seems really nice."

"Oh, yeah, Morgan's great."

"You don't think it's...awkward that she's gay though?" Raven broached the subject carefully.

Summer frowned . "No. Why should it matter?"

"I'm not saying it does. I'm just...doesn't it bother you, even a little, that she makes out with other girls?"

Summer's frown deepened. "No, it doesn't. I had no idea you were such a homophobe."

"I'm not. Summer, I'm not. I like Morgan, okay? It's just..." She shrugged, not quite sure what she was getting at. She certainly couldn't tell Summer that she'd imagined what it would be like kissing another girl after learning Morgan was gay. "Never mind, all right?"

Chapter Five

By eleven, Raven was ready and on the road to the university. Mid-morning traffic was light, and she made good time, arriving ten minutes before their scheduled meeting. This was even with the stop she made for coffee and pastries. It took her a few minutes to find a parking spot, and she got turned around a couple of times making her way across the campus to the library, so by the time she found Morgan in the study carrels, she was no longer early, nor was she late, exactly.

Morgan looked up as she approached and offered a smile. "Hey. You find your way okay?"

"I managed," Raven said as she slid into the chair across from her. She didn't want to admit that she'd gotten lost even if it was probably fairly obvious she had. She'd been on campus a few times before, but she'd never had to navigate her way around. Julia had been around to play guide.

"I come bearing gifts," she added, opening her messenger bag and pulling out the wrapped Danish she'd bought earlier. The coffee was long gone, and there was really no way she would have been able to sneak it inside anyway, but she'd saved the pastries to share. After a quick glance around to make sure nobody was in sight, she carefully unwrapped the bag and placed it on the table between them. "Breakfast of champions."

"Breakfast?"

"Well, more like brunch now, I guess. But it's the thought that counts, right?" She offered a winning smile and Morgan laughed softly.

"I suppose. And it has been a while since breakfast."

Raven glanced at her watch then at Morgan. "What time did you get up this morning?"

"Six."

"As in, a.m.? On a Saturday?"

"Yeah, I wanted to get some time in at the studio before we met."

"There is something wrong with you," Raven said with a shake of her head.

"Just get your books out."

With a roll of her eyes, Raven dug into her bag and pulled out the textbook and her binder of notes and previous tests. Wordlessly, she handed them over to Morgan and averted her eyes as Morgan began flipping through. She was embarrassed for Morgan to know how badly she'd been doing in class and had the overwhelming urge to tell Morgan that the rest of her grades were good, that she was doing well in her other subjects. It was ridiculous, really, because Morgan already knew she was failing—that's why they were here. That didn't stop the blush from heating her cheeks as Morgan let out a soft, "ouch" at one of her test scores and winced at another.

"I know, right?" she said, trying to shrug it off.

Morgan glanced up at her. "Don't take this the wrong way, but why are you even in this class?"

The wrong way? Was there a right way to take a question like that? Because as far as Raven could tell, it stung any way you took it.

"I needed an art credit. And if you think this is bad, you should hear me try to play an instrument." It had come down to the fact that art history was the lesser of two evils when compared to her other option, music theory and composition. At least in this class she could fail quietly instead of out loud and in front of her peers.

"Right. Got it." Morgan fell silent as she opened the textbook.

"Are you having second thoughts? Because if you don't think you can help, that's fine. No big deal."

"Raven, relax." Morgan reached out and laid a hand over Raven's. "I can help. I just need a minute to figure out the best way to work with you, okay?"

Raven nodded mutely, unable to think or form words as she stared down at where Morgan's fingers rested against her skin. Tracking her gaze, Morgan stiffened and pulled back. It took a moment for Raven's brain to catch up to the situation, and when it did, she felt like a first-class jerk. Now Morgan probably thought she *was* some kind of homophobe, like Summer had last night.

"I'm sorry," she said with a sigh. "I'm being a jerk. I'm stressed and I'm taking it out on you, and you really don't deserve it."

"It's all right."

"No, it's not. You're giving up your Saturday for me, and the least I can do is be grateful."

"No, the least you can do is pass your exam so today won't turn out to be a huge waste of my time," Morgan said with a smile that took the sting out of her words.

Raven nodded. "Okay. I put myself in your capable hands."

"Uh-huh." Morgan didn't actually roll her eyes, but the tone of her voice managed to give the impression that she had.

It broke the tension that had settled between them, though, and brought Raven back to the issue at hand. She leaned forward, listening carefully as Morgan laid out a study plan.

❖

By the time they called it quits for the day, Raven was actually feeling confident that, while she might not ace the exam, she would at least be able to pass it. All thanks to Morgan.

"You're in pretty good shape," Morgan was saying as Raven gathered up her things and shoved it all back into her bag. "You've got a grasp on the different artists and their styles. Tomorrow, I'll bring in a bunch of paintings and we'll work on your interpretations of them."

"Tomorrow?" Raven paused in her movements and glanced over at Morgan. "What? No. You've already given up your Saturday to help me. I can't ask you to waste your whole weekend."

"Do you want to pass this test or not?"

"Of course I do. But—"

"Then you need another day to study. It's just one more day, okay? Is it really *so* bad spending time with me?" she teased her.

Raven rolled her eyes and relented, knowing Morgan was right. Another day of cramming would do her a lot of good. And the thought of getting to spend some more time with Morgan was rather appealing as well.

• 26 •

"I suppose I can stand another day with you," she said with a heavy sigh. Then put all joking aside to thank Morgan for her time and effort.

"Of course."

"You've got to let me pay you back," she added.

"You can do that by passing your test."

That wasn't really what Raven meant. Morgan had done something for her, and Raven wanted to do something in return. "Let me buy you dinner." It was the only thing she could think to offer.

"You really don't have to."

"C'mon, you've got to eat, right? You can stand my company long enough for a free meal can't you?"

Morgan laughed softly. "All right. Let's go."

CHAPTER SIX

Since Morgan knew the area, Raven let her pick the restaurant. She chose a Chinese place a few blocks off campus, and Raven readily agreed. They bundled up in their coats and scarves and headed outside.

It had been morning when Raven stepped into the library, and night had fallen while they were inside. It was a little disorienting to walk out into cold darkness, and she was content to be following Morgan's lead at the moment. They walked quickly, hands stuffed into pockets, hats pulled down low over their ears, and within a few minutes, they stepped into the warmth of the restaurant.

They were greeted by an elderly Asian man who grinned and nodded at them as he showed them to a booth in the corner before disappearing into the back room without a word. Raven slid onto the padded bench and glanced around, taking the place in. Paper lanterns were strung across the ceiling, and rice paper scrolls depicting waterfalls and paintings of dragons dotted the walls. Incense burned at the center of each table, and music played softly in the background. There were maybe two dozen booths and tables, and over half of them were full—a mixture of families and college kids.

"Nice place."

"Yeah. It's close to campus and it's cheap."

"I hope that's not the reason you chose it." Raven hadn't expected Morgan would take her somewhere outrageously expensive or anything, but she hadn't wanted her to pick the cheapest place she could find, either.

"It's not. The food is good."

Raven caught her eye and held it, trying to determine if she was lying. When Morgan held her gaze firmly, she figured she was probably telling the truth and let it go.

"You know, I'd never had Chinese food until I came here for school," Morgan said. "Then Jules and a couple others brought me here one night, and now I'm in here at least once a week. I think I've eaten everything on the menu, probably more than once."

"Seriously?"

"What, that I'm in here that much or that I'd never eaten it before?"

"Well, both, actually. But I was thinking more that you'd never had it before. How is that even possible?"

"There weren't any Chinese restaurants in town. I guess from never having it, it wasn't something I ever wanted."

Raven shook her head, unable to fathom growing up and never eating Chinese food. It had been a staple around her house. Though that probably had more to do with the hours her mom had worked as a nurse and her father's unfailing ability to burn anything that wasn't barbequed than anything else. That didn't stop her from gently teasing Morgan about her "deprived upbringing."

The arrival of the waiter interrupted their conversation, and once they'd placed their orders and he departed, they moved on to other topics. They chatted easily over dinner and dessert and lingered long after their plates had been cleared away.

It was only as the wait staff began tipping the empty chairs up onto the tables and sweeping the floors around them that Raven glanced at her watch and realized they'd been there for almost three hours and the place was closing up.

"I guess it's time to call it a night," she said, feeling reluctant to do just that.

Morgan glanced down at the watch on her own wrist and let out a murmur of surprise. "Wow, I had no idea it was so late."

"Time flies and all that," Raven said with a shrug as they stood and gathered their things.

"Apparently."

The walk back to campus was quiet and brisk, the cold driving them on and bringing their conversation to a necessary halt. Even though Raven was reluctant for the night to end, she was grateful when they came upon the lot where she'd parked and the imminent warmth of the inside of her car. With frozen fingers, she dug into her bag for her keys and hit the button to unlock the car.

"Thanks for today," she said, turning to Morgan before opening her door. She meant for more than just the tutoring, and she hoped Morgan understood that.

"No problem. I had fun. Now, please go before I freeze to death out here."

Raven laughed. "See you tomorrow."

Morgan surprised her by stepping in for a quick hug. As Morgan's arms came around her shoulders, Raven's heart ceased beating and her breath caught in her throat, even as her own arms came up to encircle Morgan's waist, an automatic response. Then she was relaxing into the embrace, almost melting into Morgan's arms, and had to bite her lip to prevent a contented sigh. It was Morgan who pulled away first, stepping back with a squeeze of her shoulders and an easy smile.

"Night, Raven."

Chapter Seven

Raven wasn't much of a morning person. She could manage to make herself get out of bed during the week for school because she had to, but even that was a lengthy struggle of snooze buttons and bargaining with her schedule for every possible extra moment of sleep. When the weekends finally rolled around, she relished the chance to lie in bed for a couple of extra hours. Which is why she felt a little disconcerted to find herself not only awake but ready to get out of bed at seven fifteen on a Sunday morning. She had set her alarm for nine the night before, figuring that would give her plenty of time to hit the snooze once or twice and still be able to get ready and make it to the university. Instead, she found herself lying awake in bed feeling restless and having no interest in trying to fall back asleep so she rolled out of bed and got ready for another day of studying with Morgan.

❖

Raven found Morgan at the same table in the library, textbooks spread out around her, though her attention was focused on the novel in her hand. She didn't appear to notice

Raven's approach. She didn't even look up when Raven reached the table and was standing directly in front of her. Holding back a smile, she gripped the chair in front of her and pulled it out slowly and then dropped into it. The sudden movement caught Morgan's attention, and she jumped. Her book fell out of her hand as she let out a yelp of surprise. Luckily, the library was nearly empty, with only a few other students on the far side of the room, because Raven burst out laughing.

"You are such a brat," Morgan muttered as she leaned to retrieve her book.

"Sorry."

"Yeah, you sure sound it."

"No. I really am."

"And I might believe you if you'd wipe that smirk off your face."

Raven tried to school her expression but couldn't keep her grin at bay. "Peace offering?" She held up the bag of brownies she'd picked up from the same coffee shop as yesterday.

Morgan appeared to consider for a moment before letting out a sigh and reaching for the bag. "Ready to get started?"

They spent the next couple of hours going through the various textbooks Morgan had brought, analyzing different pieces of artwork. Raven listened as Morgan described each piece, trying to see what she saw. But for all Morgan's talk of brushstrokes and symmetry and negative space, Raven mostly just saw shapes and colors. She saw trees and flowers and a boy in blue and not much more, but the passion in Morgan's voice as she explained each piece, the obvious regard she had for the work, made Raven want to do better, so she struggled through, trying to find the same beauty, and eventually, she started to see it. She started to see the elements of each piece, as opposed to just the final product. She started to recognize shadow and light, and space, and the use of color. She doubted she would ever have the same appreciation for art that Morgan did, but she was beginning to see her perspective.

❖

"You know what? I think you've got it," Morgan said after Raven had finished her fourth analysis without any prompting.

"You think?" she asked, feeling both proud and disappointed.

"Oh, yeah. I think you're in good shape for your exam."

"That's good." And it was. Yet she couldn't seem to muster up any enthusiasm at the thought. She knew she should be excited that she wasn't going to fail, but all she could think about was that her time with Morgan was coming to an end.

"It is," Morgan agreed as she stood and began to gather up the books. Reluctantly, Raven stood as well and helped Morgan return them to their places on the shelves.

"You hungry?" Morgan asked as they returned to the table for their things. "Want to get lunch?"

Raven immediately agreed. She wasn't particularly hungry, but she'd take any excuse to spend a little more time with Morgan.

❖

It was snowing when they left the library, fat, fluffy flakes that coated their hair and shoulders within minutes. The ground was already covered in a thin layer of white. It was a short walk across campus to a coffee shop that Morgan promised made the world's best wraps, but they were still covered in snow when they got there.

"I feel like the abominable snowman," Raven commented as she brushed snow from her bangs and stomped her boots against the welcome mat just inside the door.

"And you look like it, too," Morgan said as she shook out her curls.

"Like you're any better."

"But at least my coat isn't wool," Morgan reminded Raven as she reached over and began brushing snow off her shoulders and arms. It wasn't even a solid touch, just a light sweep of fingers against fabric, but still, she flinched. Luckily, Morgan didn't seem to notice as she continued her ministrations.

Raven held herself stiffly, muscles tense as her heart stuttered then picked up a rapid pace. A warm flush heated her cheeks, and she hoped her already cold-reddened face hid the blush.

"You're lucky it didn't soak through," Morgan said, oblivious to her discomfort. After one final last brush, she stepped back, and Raven was able to breathe again. On shaky legs, she followed Morgan across the coffee shop to the counter and took her place in line beside her.

As Morgan perused the menu board, Raven tried to puzzle out what had just happened.

"Raven. Hey." An elbow in her side made her realize she was being spoken to. She shook her head, trying to clear it.

"Sorry, what?" She glanced over at Morgan then at the guy behind the counter, both of whom were giving her amused glances.

"Are you ordering?"

She blushed, realizing that while she was spaced out, they'd made it to the head of the line. She glanced up at the menu, which she hadn't even looked at yet and tried to read it quickly.

"Just give her what I'm having," Morgan told the guy as she took Raven by the elbow and steered her toward an empty booth along the wall. "What's with you?" she asked as they slid onto opposite benches.

Raven shook her head. "Nothing."

"Nothing? You completely zoned out on me."

Raven blushed. "It's nothing. I don't know."

Morgan gave her a long, measuring look so Raven decided to distract her before she could pursue it. "So, just what did you order for me, anyway?"

The rest of their lunch passed pleasantly and was over much too soon for Raven's liking. It felt like minutes but was actually over two hours that they lingered over turkey wraps and coffee refills. The midday rush came and went while they talked about school and movies and music and friends, and still Raven wished they could stay longer. But three cups of coffee was her limit in one sitting, and the snow was starting to pick up. She didn't want to get stuck in a blizzard on her way home. So reluctantly, she said she needed to be going.

Morgan insisted on walking her back to her car, even though it was in the opposite direction of her dorm. Raven knew she should decline and let her get out of the cold, but she accepted anyway, eager for another few minutes of company.

They walked quickly and without conversation, the snow crunching lightly beneath their boots. The campus was quiet, not a single soul in sight.

"I can't thank you enough for all this," Raven said as they reached her car. "And it's been great getting to hang out."

"Yeah. Definitely. Your test is tomorrow, right?"

"Nine a.m."

"You'll call me; let me know how it goes?"

"Sure. Yeah." Raven pulled her cell phone out of her pocket and flipped it on. As soon as it had powered up, she opened a new contact for Morgan's number, feeling disproportionately pleased by the thought of talking with Morgan again. She keyed in the information and tucked her phone back into her pocket.

"So, I'll talk to you later," Raven said, feeling a little awkward but trying to ignore it.

"I look forward to it. Drive safe."

Before she could reply, Morgan had stepped in for a hug.

When Morgan pulled back, Raven felt a surge of disappointment. The next thing she knew, she had tipped her head forward and was pressing their lips together. Then she was reeling backward, heart racing and feeling light-headed, trying to figure out what she'd just done.

"Raven—"

"I've got to go." Unable to look Morgan in the eye, she climbed into her car and jammed the key into the ignition.

"Raven." Morgan's voice was muffled through the glass of the window, and Raven ignored it as she started the wipers to clear the windshield of snow. "Don't go. We should talk about this."

Raven didn't want to talk. She revved the engine and Morgan stepped back. Raven drove away without a backward glance.

CHAPTER EIGHT

The house was in darkness when Raven pulled into the driveway. A blessing and a curse. On one hand, she wasn't in any shape to deal with people, least of all her parents. On the other, she didn't want to be alone with her thoughts right now either. The hour-long trip home had been bearable because she'd had to focus on her driving so she wouldn't end up in a ditch or something. Now, though, there was nothing to concentrate on and her thoughts would be free to wander.

With a sigh, she climbed out of her car and headed up the walk. Once inside, a detour into the kitchen revealed a note on the fridge informing her that her parents had gone to dinner with her aunt and uncle and wouldn't be home until late, but there was spaghetti in the fridge if she was hungry.

"Great. Just great." She crumpled the note and tossed it into the trash. For lack of anything better to do, she opened the fridge and examined its contents. There was the promised spaghetti, as well as the makings of a sandwich, and a crisper full of fruits and vegetables. The thought of food made the knot in her stomach clench tightly. She let the door swing shut and wandered into the living room, where she flopped onto the couch and reached for the remote. Sunday night had to be good for some cheesy made-for-TV movie she could lose herself in for a while, so she wouldn't have to think about Morgan. Or the fact that she'd kissed her.

She flipped through the channels, hoping with each click that she'd land on something that would occupy her brain for a while, so she wouldn't have to think about the fact that her lips still tingled from the brief contact, and that it didn't take any effort at all to remember the way it had felt. The warmth of Morgan's breath against her skin, the softness of her lips, and the way they'd tasted faintly of coffee. Or the way that even as she had pulled back, horrified by what she had done, all she'd really wanted to do was lean back in.

She wasn't ready to face what it meant. Not yet.

The ringing telephone saved her from having to.

"Hello?"

"Hey. Where have you been? I've been calling your cell all day."

She dug into her pocket for her cell phone and flipped it open. It had been off while she was in the library studying, and all her calls had gone straight to voice mail. Sure enough, when she checked her messages, there were six missed calls, four from Chloe, and two from Morgan. She deleted the messages without bothering to listen to them.

"Sorry, I was out."

"Yeah, I got that. Out where?"

"Studying."

Chloe let out a laugh. "Seriously, where were you?"

"Seriously, I was studying. A friend of Julia's offered to help me get ready for my art exam."

"God, you suck," Chloe groaned. "You blow me off all weekend and I can't even get mad at you for it because you were studying."

Raven couldn't help but laugh. "I'll make it up to you next weekend.

"How?"

"However you want. Dinner? On me. A movie night? I'll even watch one of those sappy romantic comedies you love so much."

"And have you ruin my enjoyment of it? I'll pass, thanks."

"Well, whatever you want, let me know. The whole weekend, I'm yours."

"Right, like I'd want to spend two whole days with you," Chloe scoffed. Raven chuckled and settled more comfortably on the couch, letting herself get pulled into inane banter with Chloe until Chloe's mom started yelling at her to get off the phone because it was a school night.

"I guess I've got to go. See you tomorrow?"

"Yeah. We'll get lunch after exams."

Raven heard Chloe's mom in the background, asking her if she had any idea what time it was.

"Yeah. Text Summer. I've really got to go."

"Night," Raven said through her laughter.

"Love you."

"You too," Raven said, the words spoken to a dial tone. Chloe had already hung up. The words carried a bitter taste with them. Would Chloe still love her if she knew what Raven had done?

Not that she had any intention of telling her friends about any of it. A wave of nausea rolled over her just at the thought of it. Who knew what their reactions would be? They might hate her, might never want to see her again.

And what about the other kids at school if they found out? She'd seen the way people treated Mitch Abernee, just because he dressed well and was more interested in photography and the drama club than sports and cars. She'd heard the names he was called behind his back, seen the way some of the jerkier guys on the football team hassled him in the hallway. And what about Lyndsey Ford? People were always calling her a dyke and making snarky comments about her staring at them in the change room after gym class just because she played on a bunch of sports teams.

If that was how they were treated, even though neither one of them had ever given any kind of indication that they were…she shook her head, refusing to contemplate it any further. Nobody would ever find out about this. They couldn't. Raven wouldn't be able to survive it if they did.

Chapter Nine

Nerves over her exam pushed aside any lingering unease from the night before, and by the time she made it to school, the kiss with Morgan had been pushed from the forefront of her mind.

When the exam papers were laid in front of her, it took all her effort and concentration to calm her racing heart and focus her thoughts to recall everything she and Morgan had reviewed over the weekend. She worked slowly through the first few questions, gaining confidence as she went, until by the end she was answering with ease.

It was the first time she'd walked out of the art room feeling confident about the work she'd turned in. She rode that sense of accomplishment for the rest of the morning, right up until she reached her house and spotted a familiar figure sitting on the porch steps.

Then last night came crashing down around her, and she paused at the end of the front walkway before slowly starting up it toward the waiting Morgan.

"Morgan," she greeted her when she reached the foot of the steps. Raven was unable to meet Morgan's eyes, or even look directly at her for more than a moment. When she looked at her, she remembered, and when she remembered, she felt that familiar warmth heating her cheeks and sending her stomach fluttering.

"I called you a couple of times last night."

"I had my phone off."

She didn't know if Morgan believed her or not, but she didn't press.

"We need to talk."

Raven shifted from one foot to the other and shoved her hands into her coat pockets. She didn't want to talk. She didn't see what talking would accomplish. Not when she'd already decided the kiss was nothing. But Morgan had been camped out on her porch steps for who knows how long, and she didn't show any indication of leaving any time soon.

"Fine. But come inside," she added, belatedly realizing Morgan must be freezing. It was minus two, or something like that.

Morgan rose, and Raven eased past her, careful not to brush shoulders or bump into her as she mounted the steps and unlocked the door. Morgan followed her silently into the house, shedding her boots and hanging her coat on the indicated rack, then trailing her into the kitchen. She leaned against the counter as Raven pulled mugs down from the cupboard and set about making coffee. It would warm Morgan, and it gave Raven something to do with her hands.

"Here," she said.

Morgan accepted a steaming mug and cradled it in her hands. Raven stared into her own, waiting for Morgan to say whatever it was she'd come here to say.

"You can't do that."

Startled, Raven glanced up.

Morgan's voice was soft but edged with an anger that shocked Raven. "I'm not an experiment, a guinea pig to test out what it feels like to kiss a girl."

"I didn't...I wasn't..."

"You didn't what? Didn't kiss me?" Morgan set her coffee down on the table and took a step closer to Raven. "No. Don't do that. You can't blame this on me."

"I'm not. I just—"

"Just because I'm gay doesn't mean I was hitting on you."

"I know that." In all her discomfort and unease around Morgan, it hadn't been because of something Morgan had done. She had never once thought Morgan was coming on to her.

"I hugged you, yes. But you kissed me."

"Morgan, I know."

"You can't just do that."

"I know. I'm sorry."

"If you know, then why did you?"

Raven cut her gaze away from Morgan and let her eyes travel the room as she struggled to come up with an explanation, a reason for her behavior. She could tell Morgan was getting impatient, could hear the scuffle of her socked feet as she shifted.

"Raven?"

"Because...I think I might be gay."

Chapter Ten

From the expression on her face it was obvious that wasn't what she'd expected Raven to say. The words hung heavy in the air between them. This was the first time Raven had said it aloud, had even allowed herself to fully form the thought. But in saying the words, it was like all of the pieces of the puzzle had slid into place. Some of the little things that had confused her before suddenly made sense. Like why the few dates she'd been on had been fun, but anything even remotely physical had made her vaguely uncomfortable. She'd always found a reason to pull her hand away or move out from beneath his arm. And waiting for that good-night kiss had been more stressful than pleasant. She had tried very hard not to examine what it meant and played it off as the spark just not being there. She couldn't deny it any longer.

"You're gay?" Morgan asked, not even bothering to hide her skepticism.

Raven nodded. "I think…I'm pretty sure."

Saying it for the first time had been awkward and strange, the words forming uneasily on her tongue, but it had also been a relief to say it out loud, to finally acknowledge the truth she had been avoiding for so long. Repeating it, however, was simply terrifying. As the weight of the words settled around her shoulders, all Raven could feel was a growing sense of panic. She wasn't naïve; she knew the struggles gay people faced. She didn't want that.

Tears pricked at her eyes, and she blinked rapidly to keep them at bay. Morgan's expression softened, sympathy replacing anger as she closed the distance between them and gently guided her toward the table.

"Let's sit." She pulled out one of the chairs, and Raven fell gracelessly into it.

"How long have you known?"

"A while, I guess." Raven gripped her coffee mug with both hands, staring down into the steaming liquid as if it could provide her with answers or an explanation. "But I didn't want to know. Didn't want to admit it."

She explained, or tried to explain, how she'd always felt just a little out of step with her friends, how she'd always known she was different despite every effort to be the same. How she'd hoped, if she just kept going through the motions, eventually things would fall into place. That if she talked about guys with her friends and went out on dates then eventually she would find one she liked.

Morgan listened silently, squeezing her wrist or patting her hand when she faltered, and despite the tears threatening to spill over and the tightening of her chest as the truth settled deeper, she still felt a fluttering in her stomach at Morgan's touch.

Raven didn't want to tell Morgan that she was the catalyst: meeting her and spending time with her had undone all of the carefully crafted excuses and denials. In part, she was afraid if she voiced it, she'd get angry with Morgan for her role in things, even though she knew it wasn't really her fault. Also, she was afraid if she told her, Morgan would stop holding her hand.

"I'm sorry I kissed you," she finished "I didn't mean to. I mean, I didn't plan it. But I knew you were gay, and I just…I had to know."

"What it felt like to kiss a girl?

"Whether I liked it."

"And you did."

"Yeah. I'm sorry I used you like that. I know it wasn't fair."

Morgan's fingers tightened around her own. "It's okay."

Raven was glad Morgan wasn't still mad at her. She was also starting to feel guilty that she was enjoying Morgan's touch so much. With a sigh, she leaned back in her chair, her hand sliding from beneath Morgan's as she did.

Her thoughts were a confused jumble. How could she be so freaked out at the thought of being gay, at the whole idea of being with another girl, going out on dates, holding hands, kissing, yet be attracted to Morgan at the same time?

"Hey, what are you thinking?" Morgan leaned forward, her elbows resting on the table as her hand sought out Raven's once again.

The touch sent a jolt coursing up her arm, and she let out a shaky breath. She knew Morgan was just trying to make her feel better, but Morgan's touch was not helping her confusion any.

"I'm thinking my parents are going to freak out. That my friends are never going to talk to me again. That my life, as I know it, is over." And it was all true. It just wasn't the whole truth.

"Okay, take it one step at a time." Morgan's voice was low and soothing, but combined with the way her thumb was gently stroking the tops of Raven's knuckles, it was also stirring up feelings that were just too hard to take. Once again, she pulled her hand from Morgan's grasp, this time running her fingers through her hair.

"You've just figured things out for yourself. That's not saying you have to tell everyone right away."

Raven's heart lifted at that. She didn't have to tell anyone. She could just keep going the way she had been. That way her family wouldn't disown her and her friends wouldn't hate her.

"Give yourself some time to adjust to the idea," Morgan continued. "When you feel comfortable with it yourself, then you can come out to your family and friends."

Raven nodded, though she saw no reason why anyone else had to know.

"You can't keep it a secret forever," Morgan added, as if reading her mind. "What? You think I didn't want to do the exact same thing?"

Raven shrugged and offered a sheepish grin.

"It'll start to eat away at you if you keep it to yourself for too long. As hard as it can be to come out, it's easier than hiding."

Raven had a little trouble believing that.

"I was terrified to come out. I thought my parents were going to kick me out and my friends were going to hate me, but after I'd kept it a secret for almost a year, it started to get to me. I was depressed and angry all the time. I had to tell my parents."

"And?"

"And they took it really well. It shocked them, of course, and things were a little awkward for a while. My mom tried so hard to be understanding, and my dad got tense every time I had a friend over who was a girl, but they mellowed out. Things are good now."

"And your friends?"

Morgan broke eye contact, and Raven felt her heart sink.

"I only told a few people, some friends and a couple of kids from my art classes. Most of them were fine with it, but my best friend…"

Raven had heard enough. She wasn't ready to hear details on that part. "You don't have to tell me if you don't want to talk about it."

"I'm sorry. I didn't mean to freak you out."

"You didn't."

Morgan raised an eyebrow.

"Okay, you did. I'm definitely freaking out right now, but if you want to tell me, I can take it." It was the least she could do, given how much Morgan had done for her. First with helping her study, and now being so supportive. If Morgan needed a sympathetic ear, Raven could be that.

"Thank you. But I've dealt with it. I have a lot of other really good friends who do accept me."

Raven nodded. "That's good. I'm glad." Although what Morgan had told her wasn't entirely reassuring, Raven felt better. The thought of coming out to her family, her friends, still seemed terrifying, but having Morgan here telling her this wasn't the end of the world, it helped.

CHAPTER ELEVEN

Raven thought she'd feel different after her admission, but she still felt like her same old self. She looked the same too. After Morgan left, she'd spent twenty minutes staring at herself in the bathroom mirror, looking for some sort of change in her features but found nothing different. People weren't going to be able to look at her and know. It was a relief, and yet she still felt nervous as she mounted the steps of Chloe's front porch and rang the bell. Butterflies erupted in her stomach as she heard footsteps approaching from within the house. The door swung open, and even though Raven was expecting it, she jumped. Chloe noticed and laughed but, to Raven's relief, didn't question it.

"You made it," she said as she reached out and tugged Raven inside by the wrist. "Everyone else is already here."

Raven flinched at the contact, her breath catching in her throat as Chloe's fingers pressed against the skin of her wrist. Was this okay? Was she allowed to touch and hug her friends now that she was…gay? Even in her head, she stuttered over the word.

Chloe didn't appear to notice her discomfort as she guided Raven down the hall toward the basement rec room where everyone was gathered.

They made it downstairs, and Chloe finally dropped her hand so she could return to her place beside AJ on the couch. Raven took her first deep breath since she'd entered the house as she dropped gracelessly onto the other couch beside Summer.

"You're late."

"And apparently I've missed so much." She gestured with a smirk to the textbooks sitting unopened on the coffee table in front of them and then to the magazine in Summer's hand.

"We were waiting for you."

"Well, I'm here now."

"Yeah, I can see that," Summer said, then went right back to her magazine. Raven laughed and grabbed a magazine of her own from the pile then settled more comfortably against the cushions.

"Hey, Rae, what do you think, hotter with dark hair or the blond highlights?" Summer's voice in her ear startled her, and she jumped, dropping her magazine to the floor with a dull thud.

"Someone's jumpy today," Summer said with a laugh as she slid even closer, her hip bumping Raven's, their shoulders brushing. She bent and picked up the magazine, placing it in Raven's lap before going back to her question.

"What do you think? Hot or not?"

Raven stared at her then flicked her gaze to the photo and stared without really seeing as she tried to figure out how to answer the question.

They'd had this conversation dozens of times before... doesn't she look so pretty in that dress? Isn't she beautiful? Don't you think she looks gorgeous with her hair long like that? Time and time again, they'd flipped through fashion and gossip magazines, scrutinizing outfits and making comments without a second thought. But it felt dangerous this time, as if she might give herself away by making the wrong comment.

"I know, right? I can't decide either," Summer said with a shrug and turned her attention back to the page in front of her.

Raven slumped back against the couch, feeling deflated. She had dodged a bullet this time, but what about the next time? Or the time after that? She would always have to watch her words and expressions. She'd have to be on guard all the time. Just the thought of it was exhausting. And she hated it. After a decade of friendship, all of a sudden she couldn't be herself. She felt tense and awkward when they got too close. She questioned every comment, every gesture, noting things she never would have given a second thought to before.

Like the fact that Summer had not slid back to her place at the other end of the couch but had remained where she was, very much invading Raven's personal space. A week ago, it wouldn't have even registered, but right now all Raven could think about was how Summer's elbow brushed her side every time she turned a page and how her foot tapped the back of Raven's leg rhythmically. Summer probably didn't even realize she was doing either of these things, but Raven felt each brush of contact with an uneasy tension. She wondered if Summer would feel so comfortable sitting next to her if she knew the truth.

She'd seemed okay with the fact that Morgan was gay. She'd even gotten a little angry when she thought Raven wasn't. But that was different. Morgan wasn't her best friend since kindergarten. And Raven had no idea where Chloe stood on the subject.

She couldn't bear the thought of losing them, especially because of something over which she had no control. But at the same time, she wasn't sure how long she could go on keeping this secret from them. Not when it was taking up so much space in her head.

How long could she really go on jumping at every touch, tensing when they got too close, weighing every word? She was relieved when they ended their "study break" and went back to work, but she still couldn't relax entirely. Because even though she couldn't get into trouble talking about Shakespeare or helping Summer work through equations, she knew it was just a matter of time before she blundered. All it would take was one comment, one touch when she wasn't prepared for it, and she'd give herself away. Then what? Would she lose two of the most important people in her life? Would she be outed at school? It was all too much to deal with.

A couple of hours later when Chloe unceremoniously kicked them out so she could have dinner with her boyfriend, Raven was, probably for the first time ever, eager to leave Chloe's house.

Chapter Twelve

R aven did her best to avoid everyone over the course of the rest of the week. She spent most of her time holed up in her room "studying," skipping meals, and dodging phone calls so she wouldn't have to deal with her parents or her friends. It was too hard for her to be around people right now, to listen to them talk and joke and laugh without a care in the world while she was carrying this big secret. Even though she wasn't ready to tell anybody yet, she felt guilty for lying— or at least withholding—and she resented having to be careful about what she said and how she acted.

Her one bright spot, the thing that kept her from going completely crazy in the midst of her self-imposed isolation, was the dinner plans she had made with Morgan on Friday night. The thought of spending time with someone who knew her secret, someone she didn't have to be on guard around, was immensely appealing. And it provided her with an excuse as to why she wouldn't be spending the evening with her friends. When the text came—as she'd known it would—inviting her to dinner and a movie, she had an answer ready.

Her phone buzzed a few times as she drove up to the university, but she ignored it, left it lying on the seat beside her. She knew her friends were likely getting pissed at her sudden disappearing act, and she did feel guilty for avoiding them, but there really wasn't anything she could do about that. She simply couldn't be around them right now, not until she had a handle on herself.

She felt a wave of guilty relief when she reached the now familiar visitor parking lot of the university and climbed out of her car, leaving her cell phone locked inside.

All thoughts of her friends faded, however, when she turned around and spotted Morgan striding across the parking lot toward her. Raven couldn't prevent the grin that tugged at the corners of her lips any more than she could help the fluttering in her stomach when Morgan grinned back. Instantly, Morgan was upon her, arms going around Raven in a hug.

"Hey, girl. How are you holding up?" The words were a vibration against her shoulder that sent shivers down her spine.

"I'm fine," she said into Morgan's neck, trying not to notice just how close her own lips were to her skin.

"Fine?" Morgan pulled back to give her a raised eyebrow, and Raven realized the pointlessness of lying to the one person who knew exactly what she was going through.

"All right, I'm a mess," she admitted. "I can't eat. I can't sleep. I've been avoiding everybody. Whenever one of my friends touches me, I have a heart attack. And I have to spend the whole day with Chloe tomorrow." Tears built in her eyes, and she blinked them back, desperate not to turn into a wreck right now.

Morgan squeezed her hand then tugged on it gently, starting them both walking across the lot away from the school. "So for dinner, I was thinking Mexican. There's this place a couple of blocks away that I think you'll love."

Raven nodded, not trusting her voice. She was grateful to Morgan for not pushing her. As much as she appreciated having someone to talk to about what she was going through, she didn't want that to be all they talked about. She just wanted to feel normal for one night.

They made the walk in silence, hands thrust deep into coat pockets, and hats pulled down low against the cold. By the time they reached the restaurant, Raven was feeling better. She'd managed to quell her emotions and push down all the thoughts that had been weighing her down. She was determined to have a good time tonight.

"After you." Morgan pulled the door open and made a grand sweeping gesture with her hand, ushering Raven inside ahead of her.

She nodded her thanks and stepped into a total assault on her senses. An array of spices filled her nostrils, tinny mariachi music blasted from hidden speakers around the room, and neon green cacti blinked off and on at her from behind the bar.

"Oh, my God," Raven said in Morgan's ear as she glanced around. The entire place was done up in wood, exposed beams in the ceiling, sawdust-covered floors, rough-hewn tables, and booths scattered around. The walls were paneled and dotted with brightly colored sombreros and earth toned ponchos. Chili pepper lights draped across the ceiling, and a large piñata donkey hung in the center of the room.

"This place is horrible."

"It's awesome, isn't it?" Morgan grinned, and Raven bit her lip to prevent herself from bursting out laughing.

The hostess appeared and asked them to please follow her. A moment later, they were seated at a booth by the window. Their hostess introduced herself, although Raven wasn't really listening, and handed them each a menu, which Raven took absently. She was too distracted by the mariachi men salt and pepper shakers and the rest of their surroundings to concentrate.

"I think this might be my favorite place. Ever," she said when she could finally speak without laughing. "How in the world did you find it?"

The restaurant was in the far corner of a strip mall between a bank and a dollar store. It didn't seem like the kind of place many people just wandered into.

"I actually had a date here on Wednesday."

"A date?"

Raven struggled to keep her voice steady and not think too much about the knot that had formed in her stomach.

Morgan nodded. "Yeah."

"I thought you weren't ready for dating."

"Cindy wouldn't leave me alone. It seemed easier to agree than fight with her about it for the next three months."

"Okay. So, how was it?" Raven asked, not quite sure she wanted to be having this conversation, but knowing there was no way around it.

"It was okay."

"You didn't have a good time?"

"No. I had fun."

"But?"

Morgan shrugged. "I just wasn't into it."

"Because you're still not over your ex?"

Morgan averted her gaze and shrugged again. Raven would have taken it as confirmation if not for the faint blush coloring Morgan's cheeks.

"Or because you're into someone else?"

Morgan was suddenly incredibly interested in her menu, keeping her eyes glued to it instead of looking over at Raven.

"You are. You like someone. Who is it?" she asked, even though she wasn't sure she wanted to know.

"It's no one."

"You have to tell me."

The idea of Morgan dating someone was uncomfortable, but still she pushed. She felt like it was her duty as Morgan's friend to get her to confess. She might not have ever really been interested in anyone before, but she knew the signs.

"Forget about it. Let's talk about something else."

"Aww, come on, you have to tell me."

"Just drop it."

"Morgan. C'mon. Please?"

"It's you, Raven. All right? I'm attracted to you."

Raven stared at Morgan, stunned. She certainly hadn't expected that. Nor did she expect the giddiness that the words caused. She tried to speak. Her mouth opened, but no words came out. She didn't know what to say. Not when Morgan's words were causing two conflicting reactions. Knowing Morgan was interested in her was flattering, to say the least. The thought of holding her hand, hugging her, kissing her sent Raven's heart fluttering in excitement, even as the concept of being with Morgan terrified her.

"Look, Raven, I'm sorry, all right?"

"You're sorry? For what?"

"I shouldn't have said that. You have enough to deal with without me adding to it. You've been out a week and here I am hitting on you."

Had it really been only a week? It seemed like a lifetime ago.

"I'm the one who kissed you." It was the only response she could think of.

Morgan's gaze came up to meet hers, though her stare was blank as if she were still processing what Raven had said. "What?"

"Last weekend. I was the one who kissed you. Don't tell me that my kiss was so memorable you've forgotten it already?"

The joke fell flat as Morgan continued to stare at her.

"I told you I'd been questioning myself for a while, right? That I knew but hadn't really admitted it to myself."

Morgan nodded.

"Well, did you ever stop and wonder why now? Why you?"

"Because I'm the first lesbian you've met?"

"All right, that's part of it," Raven had to concede. "But mostly it's because I'm attracted to you, too. Have been since we met."

Morgan blinked at her, clearly stunned.

"It was what finally made me admit it to myself." She couldn't help but reach out and lay her hand over Morgan's, where it rested on the table.

"Raven…" Morgan's voice was a protest, a plea, but Raven barely heard it. Her focus was on the soft skin beneath her fingers and the warmth that radiated up her arm from the touch.

"We shouldn't," Morgan said, even as she turned her palm upward and laced their fingers together.

"I know the timing is wrong. But I can't deny, this feels really nice." She squeezed Morgan's hand lightly for emphasis.

"It's not a good idea," Morgan said softly, but she returned the pressure, squeezing Raven's hand lightly.

Chapter Thirteen

R aven barely tasted her food, her entire focus was on Morgan sitting across from her. All her senses were attuned to how she felt in this moment, as she stopped fighting and allowed herself to luxuriate in the attraction. She reveled in the way her stomach fluttered and her heart sped up when Morgan caught her eye and smiled. And the heat that traveled up her leg when their feet bumped beneath the table.

She'd never experienced this breathless giddiness, just from being in another person's presence before she'd met Morgan, but if this is what a crush felt like, she had a newfound sympathy for what her friends had gone through over the years. She swore never to tease them about one ever again.

Although they spent over two hours at the restaurant, lingering over dessert and coffee before finally calling it a night, it still seemed too soon when they got up to leave.

"So, decor aside, what do you think of the place?" Morgan asked as they pulled on their coats and headed out.

"This is my favorite restaurant," Raven said. "And it has absolutely nothing to do with the food," she added with a grin.

Even in the dim light of the parking lot, she could see the blush rise on Morgan's cheeks as she glanced over and gave Raven a wide smile.

"Well, aren't you charming."

Then it was her turn to blush as Morgan reached out and took Raven's hand in her own. She thought, for a brief moment, she might have a heart attack, the way it seized in her chest and then beat so loudly that it echoed in her ears.

They walked slowly back toward the campus, hands linked, shoulders brushing together with every step.

She felt a pang of disappointment when they reached the outer perimeter of the parking lot and she spotted her car silhouetted beneath the streetlight in the near distance. As if able to read her mind, or perhaps feeling the same way, Morgan's grip tightened and she stepped closer. Despite a deliberate slowing of their steps, all too soon they stood in front of Raven's car.

Without dropping her hand, Raven turned to face Morgan. She remembered the last time they'd been here in this parking lot, how she'd kissed Morgan and then run away. She didn't want to run away this time.

An expectant silence hung between them. She knew Morgan was waiting for her to make the first move, to either close the distance between them or drop her hand and climb into her car. She knew what she wanted to do. She also knew if she did, there would be no taking it back.

The first time she'd kissed her, and then run away, Morgan had forgiven her. She'd understood Raven was feeling lost and confused. If she did it a second time, she wouldn't be so understanding. If she kissed Morgan now, it would mean something. There could be no running away. She had to be sure it was what she wanted.

Using their still joined hands, she tugged Morgan forward and pressed her lips against Morgan's. As far as kisses went, it was perfect, soft and sweet, and when they pulled apart, it left her wanting more.

Raven couldn't help the grin that threatened to split her face. And from the smile Morgan was sporting, neither could she.

"That was nice," Raven said softly.

"Yeah."

Morgan leaned in and kissed her again, and it was all Raven could do to keep her legs from collapsing beneath her as she returned pressure to the lips against her own. When they pulled apart this time, she was breathless, but that didn't stop her from leaning forward and capturing Morgan's lips again. The moment was broken, though, as a car raced past on the road just a few feet away, brakes squealing as it turned the corner away from the school, making Raven realize they were making out in the middle of a parking lot. Feeling a little sheepish, she took a step back.

"I had a great time tonight." Such a cliché, but it needed to be said.

"Me, too."

"When can we do this again?" She didn't care if the question made her sound too eager.

"Tomorrow?"

Raven was about to agree when she remembered she had plans with Chloe the next day.

"I can't. I'm supposed to do something with my friend Chloe tomorrow. Sunday?"

Morgan shook her head. "I'm booked in for studio time all afternoon, and I'm meeting with my study group after dinner. Monday?"

"My dad needs the car."

Morgan let out a sigh. "And I've got late classes on Tuesday and Wednesday."

It was almost funny. Almost.

"And I've got a student council meeting on Thursday. Friday?"

"I was really hoping I wouldn't have to wait another whole week to see you," Morgan said. "But I guess it'll have to do."

Raven couldn't help but feel flattered by that. "All right then, Friday. It's a date."

She felt a shiver at the words. She had a date next Friday. A date with Morgan.

"I look forward to it," Morgan said with a smile.

"Me too."

As much as she would have loved to stay and chat with Morgan all night, she did have to be getting back.

"I'll call you later," she promised as she dropped Morgan's hand and reluctantly stepped away. She opened her car door, but before getting in turned and kissed Morgan one last time.

"One for the road," she said with a grin as she climbed in.

❖

It was late when she got home, but Raven was much too wired to sleep. She had never come home from a date feeling like this. She wanted to dance around her room in excitement. Yet, she also wanted to lie quietly and remember every moment of this evening, every glance, every touch, and most importantly, every kiss. Just thinking about Morgan's soft lips against hers sent a shiver down her spine. It was almost too much to take in.

She said a quick good night to her parents, who were watching a movie in the living room, then hurried upstairs to her room before they could draw her into a conversation. There was no way she could be around them for more than a minute or two without them realizing something was up, and she wasn't ready to tamp down this heady feeling just yet.

Alone in her room, she paced back and forth, running the evening over in her mind. The way Morgan had looked with the light from the ugly green cactus in the center of the table dancing across her features, the way she smiled whenever her eyes met Raven's across the table, and the softness of Morgan's skin when she took Raven's hand.

She became aware of the fact that her cell phone was in her hand and opened, her fingers hovering over the keypad. Hastily, she snapped it shut and tossed it onto the bed, her heart pounding in panic at what she had almost done. Her first instinct whenever anything good or bad happened was to call her friends and share it with them. She had almost done that. Summer's number had been all cued up without her even realizing it. What if Summer had answered? Would she have blurted out her secret before she was able to stop herself? Raven could feel her good mood fading, and she pushed the thoughts away before they could completely ruin her evening.

CHAPTER FOURTEEN

By the next morning, Raven's excitement had faded, dampened by the nerves she felt at facing Chloe for the first time in almost a week. Not only would she have to look her in the eye while keeping not one, but two secrets from her, she'd have to apologize and try to explain where she'd been all week.

A small part of her hoped Chloe would be too angry to want to spend the day together so she could avoid things for a little while longer. The larger part of her hated the thought of Chloe being mad at her and wanted to make things right. Or as right as they could be under the circumstances.

Her heart hammered as she rang the bell, and her breath caught in her throat as she heard the lock click. She had to force a smile onto her face as the door started to swing open. A moment later, she found herself eye to eye with Chloe, and the apology she had worked on in the car all the way over here died on her lips.

Chloe frowned mildly at her, and Raven wracked her brain for something to say, before finally settling on holding up the latte she had bought as a peace offering, hoping Chloe would take it as such.

"I'm not supposed to take gifts from strangers," Chloe said. Her tone was cold, but Raven could see the grin that was threatening to form. "Although, you do look familiar."

"I'm sorry I was a ghost all week. Exams. You know how my parents get." It was not the most eloquent of apologies, but it was the best she could manage at the moment.

A tense silence followed, and then Chloe took the cup from Raven's grasp and stepped back to let her in. "I'm not quite ready yet. C'mon upstairs."

Raven breathed a sigh of relief that Chloe opted not to turn this into a long, drawn-out thing and dutifully followed her upstairs to her room.

❖

When Chloe unbuttoned the blouse she was wearing and tossed it aside, Raven grabbed a book from the bedside table and turned it over to read the description. Even though Chloe's back was to her, Raven was not going to sit here and watch her change.

"What do you think of this shirt? Does it make my boobs look big?"

Raven froze and felt a blush heat her cheeks. This wasn't an unusual question from Chloe, who had always been a little insecure about her body. She had developed earlier than the other girls in their class, and while there were plenty who had not only caught up but surpassed her in the past couple of years, she was still self-conscious. Some of it was left over from the teasing and attention she had endured in the sixth and seventh grades, but also, she was still a bit of a tomboy. They all had been, at some point, hi-tops, baseball hats, and baggy shorts. They'd grown out of it, fashion-wise at least, but Chloe was an athlete. She played basketball and soccer and rowed and swam. She spent a lot of time being "one of the guys" and sometimes felt a little uncomfortable with her curves. Today could not have been a worse time for her insecurity to flare up, however.

"Your boobs are fine."

"You're not even looking."

Raven's blush deepened, and she kept her eyes fixed on the book in her hands. "You want me to look at your boobs?"

"Perv on me all you want. Just tell me if you think this top looks okay or not."

Chloe's comment, oddly enough, eased some of the tension that had built up inside her. It was such an offhand, easy remark that it cut through some of the discomfort she'd been feeling.

"You're the one stripping in front of me, but I'm the perv? Yeah. Okay."

She finally raised her eyes in time to see Chloe grin and give her a little shimmy. Raven rolled her eyes.

"The shirt looks good, Chlo."

"Just good?"

Raven groaned. "It looks beautiful. Amazing. Sexy as hell."

Chloe narrowed her eyes, and Raven offered her most winning smile.

"All right. Fine. Just give me five minutes to do my makeup."

"Uh-huh." Raven knew Chloe's five minutes would be more like ten, but that was all right; she was feeling a lot more comfortable than she had been when she walked through the door, and suddenly, the prospect of spending the entire day with Chloe didn't seem so daunting.

❖

"So, what exactly are we doing today?" Raven asked twenty minutes later as they climbed into Chloe's car.

"Well, I was thinking lunch at Andretti's."

"Okay." Raven drew the word out slowly, waiting for the rest of Chloe's plan. She knew it was going to be something she wouldn't like seeing as how Chloe had started off with Andretti's, which was Raven's favorite restaurant—next to the Mexican place Morgan had introduced her to.

"And then skating in the park," Chloe finished in a rush.

"Skating? C'mon, Chloe." She knew she was whining, but she couldn't help it. Of all the things Chloe could have suggested, this was probably the worst.

"We haven't gone this year, and the rink will be closing soon."

"So make AJ go with you. Isn't that part of his boyfriend duties?"

"He's at a football game with his dad."

"Chloe."

"You promised, whatever I wanted."

Chloe had her there. "Okay, fine. But when we have to spend the afternoon in the ER because I've broken something vital, no complaints out of you."

"You'll be fine."

"We'll see."

"I love you."

"Uh-huh."

It wasn't so much that she was mad at Chloe for making her go skating as she was annoyed at being tricked into it. She never would have agreed to it on her own, so Chloe had used the promise she'd made against her. She didn't hate skating—she was just really bad at it. Give her Rollerblades or a skateboard and she was fine, but put her on ice, and she was an uncoordinated mess.

Unfortunately for her, Chloe and Summer were both excellent skaters, which meant she got dragged to the outdoor rink at least once a season. Of course she made up for it in the summer when she made them go to the fair and forced them onto at least a couple of rides. All in all, it was a fair trade, but that didn't mean she had to be happy about it at the moment.

As if sensing her need to sulk for a little while, Chloe turned the radio up and they made the short drive without conversation. When they reached the restaurant, Chloe pulled into a spot near the entrance and turned to Raven with her most winning smile.

"Come on, I'm starving. Someone made me wait like an hour while they got ready." She was out the door before Chloe could come up with a reply. Chloe scrambled out after her, catching up with her just in time to step inside and be greeted by the hostess. Raven ignored the sharp jab to her ribs as she followed the woman to their table.

"They've changed the menu," Chloe commented as she scanned the cardboard placard in her hands.

"Something new?"

"Yeah, couple of things."

"As long as they didn't take away any of the good stuff," Raven said as she studied her own menu.

They spent a few minutes going over the new menu, noting the changes before falling silent as they tried to decide what they wanted.

"How hungry are you?" Chloe asked a minute or two later.

"Why?"

"Want to do appetizers?"

Raven turned her menu to the appetizer section and scanned the selection. "What were you thinking?"

"Potato skins, maybe. Or fried pickles. Or, hey, they have calamari."

"Potatoes or pickles, I'm in. But if you want to eat slimy tentacles, you're on your own."

Chloe made a face. "Well, when you put it that way…"

"Well, why do you think I put it that way?"

Chloe scowled and Raven laughed. The easy exchange, a variation of the conversation they had whenever they went out to eat, relaxed Raven further, and she found herself getting caught up in the conversation, falling into the easy banter without thinking, without weighing her words.

By the time their waitress came to take their orders, she was comfortable enough to stretch out a little, barely even flinching when her foot brushed Chloe's under the table. Chloe barely registered the contact. Her gaze flicked up to acknowledge Raven's soft apology but she didn't even pause in what she was saying. The ringing in Raven's ears subsided, the blush faded before it had even fully formed, and she slipped seamlessly back into the conversation. It wasn't until they paid their bill that Raven realized she hadn't felt awkward or cautious the entire meal.

❖

The park was packed. The parking lot was so crowded that Chloe had to pull up onto the grass because there were no empty spaces. They climbed out of the car and headed toward the outdoor rink. After renting skates, they found a space on one of the benches lining the ice to sit and pull them on. Despite her difficulty with skating, Raven was pretty good at lacing and tightening her skates and she was done before Chloe. She stood, teetering precariously, then crossed her arms and feigned impatience while Chloe fumbled with her laces.

"You suck," Chloe said as she gave her laces a final tug and then pushed herself to her feet. Raven merely smirked. "Ready?" she asked, stepping over the bench, toward the ice.

"No." Raven's smirk faded.

"Do you want me to rent you one of those cones, like the little kids use?" It was Chloe's turn to smirk.

Raven glanced up, catching site of a little boy going slowly forward and clutching a neon orange pylon for balance. She glared at Chloe.

"All right, fine." Chloe raised her hands in a mock defensive gesture, then stepped out onto the ice.

Raven followed slowly, gripping the boards for balance as she transferred her weight forward onto the skate planted on the ice. When it didn't immediately go skidding out from under her, she brought her other foot down onto the ice and shuffled out of the entryway.

"See, you're doing fine."

Raven narrowed her eyes, swearing Chloe was making her do this just for her own amusement.

Chloe's jaw worked as she fought against laughter. "Here." She reached out and took Raven's hands in her own. "Use me for balance until you get the hang of it."

Raven tensed immediately. For her part, Chloe didn't appear to notice her reaction, she just continued skating slowly backward, tugging Raven along with her. Raven tried to shake it off, tried to focus instead on forcing her legs into a fluid, gliding motion instead of noticing how soft Chloe's skin was or focusing on the point of contact of each of her fingers.

Slowly, she began to get more comfortable with the skating, and she noticed that, while the feeling of Chloe's hand over her own felt nice, warm and comfortable and familiar, it didn't bring out the butterflies the way Morgan's touch did. She didn't feel any different now, with Chloe touching her than she had a week ago. Or a month ago.

The realization, or more, the remembrance, came as a relief. Even though she was gay, her feelings toward her friends hadn't changed. She hadn't suddenly developed an attraction to Chloe just because she now realized she was attracted to girls.

CHAPTER FIFTEEN

By the time Chloe dropped her off at her house, they were cold, tired, and sore, but Raven felt better than she had in a while. For the first time in days, she was feeling like herself again, comfortable in her own body and within her own mind. She didn't know if she was just getting used to the idea of being gay or if she'd had such a nice day with Chloe, but she felt more at peace than she had in weeks.

Her parents were just getting home as well. She bumped into them coming in through the garage as she headed into the kitchen.

"Hey, honey. Just getting home?" her dad asked as he handed her one of the grocery bags he was carrying.

"Yeah. Chloe dropped me off."

"What did you guys end up doing today?" her mom asked as she set her groceries on the counter and began unloading.

"Lunch at Andretti's and then skating." She was unable to keep the grimace off her face.

"Oh, you poor girl." Her mom patted her shoulder, but her smirk belied her sympathy.

"Why didn't you invite her over for dinner?" her dad asked.

"She's going to the movies with her cousins tonight."

"So, you're stuck with the old folks on a Saturday night?"
Raven nodded.

"More like, we're stuck with her on a Saturday night," her mom teased her.

❖

While her parents began dinner preparations, Raven headed upstairs to her room. She'd been up there for barely a minute when her cell phone rang. "Hello?" She settled on her bed.

"Hey."

Morgan's voice was soft in her ear and it brought a smile to her face.

"Hey," she said, her own voice gentling. "What are you up to?"

"Well, I'm talking on the phone with you."

"Besides that, smart ass."

"Not much," Morgan said, laughing lightly. "I spent most of my day in the studio. Just got back to my dorm. What about you? How was your day with Chloe?"

"It was good," Raven said. "A few awkward moments," she added, chuckling as she remembered Chloe's request for Raven to look at her boobs. "But all in all, it went well."

"That's great. I'm glad." A slight pause and then, "Have you thought about telling her? Or your family?"

"Thought about it?" Raven let out a laugh, though there was very little humor in it. "It's all I've been thinking about."

"Easy, Rae. I'm not pushing, just asking."

Raven let out a sigh. "I know. I'm sorry."

"Hey, it's all right. I've been there. So, what did you end up doing today?"

She recounted her day, making sure to play up her utter lack of coordination on the ice. "…I'm one big bruise," she ended with.

"Well, I'm sorry I'm not there. I could kiss you all better."

Raven's throat went dry at the thought of Morgan's lips where some of those bruises were.

"Are you still there?" Morgan asked as the silence lengthened. Suddenly, she seemed to realize the unintended innuendo. "I…Oh my God, Rae. I didn't mean to…I wasn't—"

"No, it's okay. You caught me off guard but…I have to admit, it's an appealing thought."

A long moment of silence followed. "Really?"

Raven couldn't help but laugh at the incredulous tone. "Yes, really."

"I wasn't…implying anything."

"I know. I'm not even remotely ready for…that. But I like the thought of you flirting with me. I might not be very good at flirting back, at least not yet, but how am I ever going to get any better without practice?"

"Okay. But give me a smack if I start to make you uncomfortable."

"Agreed. So, what are your plans for tonight?"

"Julia and a few of us are going to the movies. Not sure what we're seeing yet, whatever's playing when we get there, I guess. What about you?"

"Not much."

"No plans tonight?"

"Not unless you count curling up in bed with some tea and a book."

"Sounds like a good night in. What are you reading?"

Raven glanced over at the books piled haphazardly on her desk, two new purchases and one on loan from Chloe. "Not sure yet."

"You're welcome to join us," Morgan said. "The theater's out in your direction. The new one, just past the water park."

Raven considered the idea. She really would like to see Morgan, but she just wasn't sure she could handle being with her in front of other people. She didn't know if she'd be able to be close to her like that and pretend she was just a friend, unable to touch her and hold her hand. But at the same time, she definitely wasn't ready to be a couple around anyone else. Especially not Summer's sister.

"Nah. I'm kind of settled in. I'm going to put on some sweats and curl up under the covers."

"What a tempting image," Morgan said, making Raven blush. "Can't say I blame you, but it would have been nice to see you." Although her words were light, easy, Raven could sense a bit of edge to them. She knew Morgan had picked up on her hesitation, and though she felt guilty about it, she was glad Morgan didn't press her on it.

"I know. I feel the same way."

"So I guess I'll let you go and get comfortable."

"Have fun tonight."

"You too. Enjoy your book."

"Call me tomorrow?"

"I look forward to it."

"Me too. Night."

Chapter Sixteen

To say she felt prepared to face school on Monday would have been overstating it a bit. Despite the success of her weekend with Chloe, skating on Saturday and then watching movies at her house on Sunday, she was still feeling apprehensive about being amongst the general population.

However, their exam grades were being handed out in homeroom today, and Raven was looking forward to seeing how she'd done, especially on her art exam, and she was eager for an excuse to talk to Morgan. Not that she needed one now that they were together. Morgan had called her twice over the weekend just to say hello, and they'd texted off and on over the past two days, so it wasn't like she couldn't just pick up the phone and dial, but she was still glad to have a reason.

Her breath caught in her throat as the teacher approached, and when he set the white slip of paper on her desk with a smile, she sat there for a long moment simply staring at it before reaching out and turning it over. Her eyes scanned the grades, seeing but not really processing until she found the one she was specifically looking for. Her art grade was the second to last one on the page: 69 percent. She resisted the urge to let out a loud whoop. It was well below the class average and a good fifteen points lower than the rest of her grades, but it was a pass and that's all she cared about.

"How'd you do?" Summer asked.

Raven handed Summer her grades and took the proffered page in return, scanning over the numbers.

"You beat me in English," Summer said, a pout in her tone.

"Yeah, but you kicked my butt in Geography."

"Huh. Yeah. I did, didn't I?"

"We tied in history," Raven pointed out, but her focus had already shifted away from the conversation as she fished into her pocket and pulled out her cell phone. Keeping it in her lap, out of sight, she flipped it open and keyed in Morgan's number.

"Probably because we used the same study notes."

Raven nodded but didn't reply as she typed out a quick message, letting Morgan know that the exam results were back and she'd call her as soon as she could.

The phone in her hand vibrated a moment later, and she glanced down to see Morgan's response, *Don't leave me hanging. Tell me now.*

Holding back a smile, she keyed in her grade.

The reply came back almost instantly: *Congratulations*.

"Hey, who are you texting?"

Raven glanced up, startled at the intrusion of Summer's voice. She'd forgotten that Summer was even there. For a moment, she debated her answer, and then decided she might as well tell the truth. Or at least as much of the truth as she could.

"Morgan. She wanted me to let her knew what I got on my exams."

Summer nodded. "So, you guys hit it off?"

Raven nodded. "Yeah. We get along really well." The truth was on the tip of her tongue. It would be so easy, just a few words, and there would be another person who knew. But the words wouldn't slip past her lips, and just the thought of telling Summer made a cold sweat break out across her brow.

"That's good," Summer said, seemingly unaware of Raven's internal struggle. "She's had a rough go of it lately. She needs good friends, you know?"

Raven nodded, not trusting herself to speak.

"We should invite her out with us sometime," Summer continued.

Raven's heart skipped a beat, and she struggled to keep her voice steady as she stuttered out an agreement. "Yeah. That would be cool."

Except the last thing she wanted was Morgan spending time with her friends. It was hard enough keeping her secret. She didn't need the added complication of hiding her relationship with Morgan when her friends were around.

The phone in her lap vibrated, indicating a message, and she tilted her head to read it, feeling suddenly self-conscious. She struggled to keep her expression neutral as she typed out a reply. Even though Summer couldn't see the screen, Raven felt awkward flirting with Morgan while her best friend sat three feet away. She was grateful when the bell rang, giving her an excuse to end the conversation with Morgan and get away from Summer. Once she was alone, Raven ducked into the rarely used bathroom beside the computer labs and pulled out her cell phone. Texting wasn't enough; she wanted to hear Morgan's voice. The phone rang once before being picked up.

"Congratulations." Morgan's voice was soft in her ear. "I'm so proud of you."

"I couldn't have done it without you."

"I wish I were there so I could give you a hug and a kiss."

Morgan's words made her heart flutter and she smiled. "I wish you were here, too."

"Friday's never seemed so far away."

Raven had to agree. The warning bell rang and she let out a sigh. "I have to go. Class is about to start."

"Call me later?"

"Of course."

CHAPTER SEVENTEEN

As Raven pulled into the parking lot, she spotted Morgan sitting on one of the bus stop benches on the far edge of the lot, waiting for her. The sight of which made her both smile and shake her head.

The lot was almost empty; only three other cars were parked within, so Raven had her pick of spaces. She coasted across the lot and pulled in beside the bench.

Morgan rose. "Hey."

"What are you doing waiting out here? You're going to freeze to death." The smile on her face only got bigger as she climbed out of her car and strode toward Morgan.

"It's not that cold out," Morgan countered as she closed the distance between them.

"It most certainly is that cold out."

Morgan's laugh came as a warm gust of air against the side of Raven's neck as her arms slid around her waist. "Then I guess I'll just have to let you warm me up."

A shiver raced down her spine at the brush of lips against her skin. Then she jumped back with a yelp as she felt an icy touch against the back of her neck.

"I thought you were going to warm me up?" Morgan reached for Raven again, trying to bury her hands under Raven's jacket. She caught the outstretched hands in her own and rubbed them briskly.

"So, what would you like to do tonight?"

"I was thinking maybe we could just hang out at my dorm," Morgan said. "Would that be all right? I was all set to take you out tonight, but then I had to buy a bunch of art supplies and now I'm all tapped out."

"Sounds good to me." The thought of getting to spend a few hours with Morgan in private, to be able to talk and flirt and sit close and hold hands without intruding eyes, was immensely appealing. They hadn't had any true alone time yet; they'd always been in public, at the library or in restaurants. It would be nice to have Morgan all to herself.

Not to mention that she completely understood being on a budget. She made good money over the summer lifeguarding at the community pool, but she had to watch her spending over the rest of the year to make it stretch.

"It does?" Morgan bit her lip, looking uncertain.

"It does."

"I was kind of hoping to do something a little more special. We're supposed to be celebrating, after all."

"It's fine. I don't care what we do as long as I'm with you. Now, come on. It's freezing." She gave Morgan's hands a tug, starting them off in the direction of the dorms.

They walked quickly, passing only a few other hardy souls similarly bundled up against the weather as they crossed campus. No one gave their clasped hands a second glance. They encountered more people as they entered the dorm building, passing by some kind of party that had spilled out into the hallway on the first floor, not to mention the steady stream of people going up and down the stairs, as they made their way up to the third floor.

Morgan exchanged greetings with a few people, nods of acknowledgement and quick hellos, but she didn't stop to talk to anybody. Raven struggled to remain steady at her side, resisting the urge to drop her hand. Although nobody really paid any attention to her beyond a few nods or polite smiles, she still squirmed under their passing glances. She felt conspicuous, wondering what the strangers thought of their joined hands.

Relief coursed through her when they finally reached Morgan's room and could slip inside, out of sight.

"Well, here it is," Morgan said with a laugh and a grand sweeping gesture. "Home sweet home."

Raven took a look around and couldn't help but chuckle as well. The room was tiny, easily half the size of her bedroom at home—maybe even smaller. A bed took up one wall, and a dresser took up most of the adjacent wall. Tucked into the corner at the foot of the bed was a bookcase crammed full of texts and binders with a TV and DVD player perched on top. A long, narrow window took up the space above. The opposite wall sported a mini fridge, a long, low desk with a beanbag chair shoved into the corner beside it, and a closet. A small throw rug spanned the few feet of open floor space between.

"No wonder you offered to tutor me. You wanted an excuse to escape this room."

"Busted." Although Morgan was grinning, Raven had a feeling she wasn't entirely kidding.

"Let me take your coat."

Raven shed her coat and handed it over.

"Grab a seat," Morgan said as she shrugged off her own coat.

A seat? Where? Raven eyed the room, taking in the desk chair piled high with notebooks and the beanbag chair, which looked well-worn and comfortable but was also piled with books, before glancing over toward the bed.

"Want something to drink?" Morgan asked as Raven gingerly took a seat on the edge of the bed.

"No. I'm fine, thanks."

"Let me know if you change your mind." Morgan stood in the center of the room for a moment, looking like she was at a loss for what to do next, and Raven couldn't help but take some comfort in her nervousness.

"How about a movie?" Morgan asked a moment later as she picked her laptop up from the desk

Raven nodded. "Sure."

"What are you in the mood for?" Morgan asked as she nudged Raven's shoulder gently so she'd slide over.

"You pick," Raven said, making room, settling herself a little more comfortably on the bed against the headboard with her legs stretched out in front of her. Morgan slid in next to her, mimicking her position as she settled the computer across her lap.

"How about…this one?" Morgan murmured to herself as she scrolled through her selections and then clicked on one.

Raven tried to lose herself in the movie, but try as she might she just couldn't seem to focus on it, her attention drawn to Morgan beside her.

Their bodies touched from shoulder to hip, and Raven thrilled at the contact. It was distracting. But she wasn't about to shift or move away. When Morgan turned her ankle, lightly bumping Raven's foot with her own, she remembered she didn't have to hold herself so carefully. She was allowed to relax. She was allowed to touch Morgan. She reached out and clasped Morgan's hand, interlacing their fingers. When Morgan squeezed her fingers gently, Raven finally relaxed into the moment.

❖

"Another movie?" Morgan asked as the credits rolled up on the screen.

Raven glanced at the computer, which now rested at the foot of the bed, and then over at Morgan. "I don't know. Would it require moving in any way, shape, or form?"

Morgan made a show of taking in their entangled position. Legs draped over each other, hands clasped, Raven's head on Morgan's shoulder. "I'm going to have to go with yes, you would have to move."

"Then, no. I don't want to watch another movie."

Raven was used to snuggling with her friends on the couch or their beds, watching movies and hanging out, Chloe's head in her lap, or Summer leaning against her shoulder, but this felt decidedly different. While just as warm and just as comfortable, this snuggle held an element of something else, something she felt only with Morgan. A deeper warmth, a longing that didn't exist when she was with her friends. She enjoyed the feeling of their heads on her shoulder or their arms around her, but she didn't miss their touch when they weren't around. She didn't want to burrow into the embrace and never let go. This, what she had with Morgan, felt intoxicating and exciting on top of all the rest.

"So I take it you're not hungry then, either."

Raven's stomach rumbled softly at Morgan's question, but she ignored it and shook her head. "Nope. Not hungry."

Beside her, Morgan's shoulders shook with silent laughter. "Liar."

She merely shrugged; there really was no refuting the accusation. She was, in fact, hungry. She let out a groan as her stomach rumbled again, this time not quite so softly. "Your fault. I wasn't hungry until you suggested it."

"Your stomach's been growling for the last twenty minutes. I'm surprised you could hear the movie over it."

Raven let out an indignant gasp even as she felt her cheeks heat, but Morgan just smiled sweetly, so she found herself unable to do anything but laugh.

"So, dinnertime. What are you in the mood for?"

"We could go for Chinese?"

Raven thought about it for a moment. It was tempting; the food was good and pretty cheap, but then she shook her head. "Can't we just grab something from the cafeteria downstairs and come back up here? We could watch that second movie or just hang out."

"Is that really what you want to do?" Morgan asked, her forehead furrowing as she frowned lightly. "You passed your exams, and it's our first real date. It should be special. It's bad enough that I couldn't take you out to a movie or something. The least I can do is take you out to dinner."

"If you really want to go out we can," Raven said "But I'd much rather grab a bite to eat and come back up here."

"You're not just saying that?"

"No. I like being like this with you." She nodded at their intertwined bodies. "And we can't very well do it in a restaurant."

Morgan nodded slightly. "All right. So, cafeteria it is." But she made no move to untangle herself from Raven.

If they were going to get up, Raven was going to have to be the one to get them moving. She waited. Nothing. "Come on, up you get." She pushed at Morgan's shoulder until Morgan half slid, half tumbled off the bed.

"Smooth," she said as Raven stood and bent to offer her hand.

CHAPTER EIGHTEEN

Admittedly, Raven didn't have much experience to compare with, but tonight was the best date she'd ever had. They'd spent the last couple of hours just sitting on the floor talking. She couldn't remember when she'd last had such a good time, and she didn't want the night to ever end, but she knew that it would have to soon. She had a curfew, and an hour drive still loomed ahead of her.

"I had a great time tonight," she said when she couldn't avoid it any longer.

Morgan glanced up at the clock on the bedside table and let out a sigh. "Me too," she said softly as she shifted across the floor to sit beside Raven. "Can I see you tomorrow?"

Raven nodded even as she realized that she already had plans. "Wait—I can't. It's my friend Noah's birthday. Summer and I are going shopping for his present and then getting ready at my house."

"Oh. That's too bad. The RAs are doing movie night in the lounge."

"Well, you know, Noah and I aren't all that close. He's really more AJ's friend than mine..."

Morgan laughed softly. "Go to your party, Raven. You know you want to."

"Yeah." It promised to be a lot of fun. It would be the first time since New Year's that her entire group of friends got together, outside of school and Noah had a pretty awesome rec room down in his basement, with a pool table and foosball and an elaborate sound system.

"What about Sunday?"

"I'm going to be in the studio all day."

Raven nodded and tried to remember her schedule for the next week and when the next free evening was. "Wednesday?"

Her parents wouldn't like her being out late on a school night, but Morgan had helped her with her exam, so if she told them she was studying they probably wouldn't object.

"I have a late class. I won't be free until about eight. But if you wanted to come after…" Morgan turned hopeful eyes on Raven.

It wouldn't be much of a visit, a couple of hours at most, but Raven didn't want to go another whole week without seeing Morgan. Texting and phone conversations just weren't the same as being there in person.

"Wednesday it is then."

"I can't wait," Morgan said softly, her gaze catching and holding Raven's. "I don't want to push you further than you're comfortable with," she said. "But I'd really, really like to kiss you right now."

A wave of warmth, of affection, rolled over Raven. Morgan asking permission was sweet—not that she needed to. Raven had been thinking about kissing Morgan all night, a combination of memory and anticipation, and she was more than ready for it now.

She couldn't help but smile as she nodded. "I'd like that."

Morgan's grin lit up her whole face as she shifted even closer.

Even though it wasn't their first kiss, it felt like it was to Raven. Her heart fluttered and her breath quickened in anticipation as Morgan leaned forward, half hovering over her as their lips gently grazed. Morgan's hand came up to rest on her hip as her own hands found their way to the back of Morgan's neck. The kiss deepened.

One of the knobs of the desk drawer dug painfully into her back, and her neck ached from the slightly awkward angle, but Raven barely registered any of this. They were vague, distant sensations compared to the warmth of Morgan's hand against her skin and the heat of Morgan's breath against her lips.

When Morgan pulled away and didn't immediately return, Raven's eyes fluttered open. Her vision cleared, and she saw Morgan still hovering over her, smiling lazily down at her.

"Hey."

"Hi."

"What's up?"

"You're really good at that."

Raven blinked at the compliment. "You're not so bad yourself," she said after a moment. She offered a teasing grin. "Did you have to kiss a lot of girls to get that good?"

Morgan arched an eyebrow. "Define a lot."

Raven gaped at her before she realized that Morgan was kidding. Or at least she hoped she was.

"Double digits?"

Raven couldn't help but laugh as Morgan made a show of counting off her fingers.

"I can count on one hand the number of girls I've kissed," she said a moment later, all traces of humor now gone from her expression. "And I've only had one serious girlfriend."

Raven honestly didn't know whether she had expected the number to be higher or lower. "Was she…how you knew you were gay?"

Morgan let out a soft sigh and shifted backward until she was leaning against the desk beside Raven. "No. Heather came later. I started to figure myself out when I was about fifteen."

Raven couldn't imagine being fifteen and dealing with this. She was barely dealing with it now.

"I was doing sets for the community theater that summer, and we had an openly gay woman in the cast. There was just something about her I was drawn to."

"Did you and she…"

"No. She was older and happily married. But it got me thinking."

Raven nodded. She knew very well what that was like.

"About three months later, there was a girl in one of my art classes, Emily. We went out a few times. Mostly just curiosity on both our parts. Neither of us had ever been with another girl before and neither of us knew anyone else who was gay. We didn't really click, and it was over before it even started. I met Heather a few months later. We dated for two years. Broke up just before I came here for school."

Raven nodded. That must have been the relationship breakup Morgan had mentioned at the dinner where they'd met.

"Then there was another girl, Sara, who I met back in September, but I just wasn't ready then. Heather was still too fresh in my mind."

She opened her mouth to ask what had happened with Heather but cut herself off as Morgan pushed herself to her feet. "You said you had to be going. I don't want you to be late and get in trouble."

The sudden shift in conversation threw her, and for a moment she just sat there, staring dumbly at Morgan's outstretched hand before reaching out and allowing Morgan to haul her to her feet. Whatever had happened was obviously still a touchy subject.

Morgan insisted on walking her to her car, so they both bundled up and headed out into the night. The short walk to her car was silent and tense, the abrupt end to their conversation hanging awkwardly between them, creating a distance even as they walked close, hands clasped and shoulders brushing with each step. She didn't know what exactly had happened, but Morgan seemed closed off now, and Raven didn't know how to reach her.

When they approached her car, Raven felt guilty at the small wave of relief that rolled through her. She pulled her keys from her pocket and then turned to Morgan.

"Thanks for a really great night."

Morgan nodded slightly.

"So, I'll see you Wednesday?" She hated how tentative the question sounded, but she felt uncertain. What if talking about her ex-girlfriend had made Morgan realize that she wasn't ready for a new one?

"I can't wait," Morgan said softly, a small smile playing at the corners of her lips.

"I'll call you tomorrow."

Raven nodded. "I'd like that."

"Night, Raven." Morgan closed the distance between them to press her lips against Raven's in a light, gentle kiss. It was quick and over nearly before it had begun, but it was enough to erase the undercurrent of tension—almost. When they pulled back, Morgan was smiling. "Drive safe. I'll talk to you tomorrow."

❖

Raven drove home in a daze, her lips still tingling from Morgan's kisses, her body still thrumming with the memory of her touch. The miles stretched out before her, but she barely noticed as her mind played the evening over and over on an endless loop. From Morgan's hug of greeting in the parking lot, to cuddling on her bed, to when their lips finally came together in a kiss. Just thinking about it set her pulse racing.

She'd never felt like this before, had never been so affected by another person, where every glance, every smile, every touch shot right down to her core. Nor had she ever been so overwhelmed by physical sensations. It was unnerving but also thrilling. For the first time in her life, she finally understood what her friends had been focused on for years, why they'd spend so much time going on about their dates holding their hands or obsessing over their first date kisses.

Her first kiss had been Corey Black at the Valentine's Day dance in the seventh grade. He'd asked her out in the middle of science class, and she'd been too stunned to do anything but agree. They'd had a good time, but when he'd kissed her after the last dance, it had been awkward and a bit of a letdown after having heard Chloe gush about how great it had been when

Brian Kale had kissed her the week before. For Raven, there had been no fireworks. No butterflies. It was so *un*-noteworthy that she hadn't even told her friends about it.

And now that she finally had someone kiss her in a noteworthy way, she couldn't tell anyone. She tried not to let that ruin her mood...but it was too late. The fluttery feeling in her stomach turned hard and heavy. The memory of how Morgan's touch made her feel grew distant, a vague concept as opposed to a moment ago when it loomed so vivid and fresh. Try as she might to recapture the sensations of the evening, she couldn't.

Chapter Nineteen

The sky outside was dark with heavy, gray clouds, and it made her want to stay cuddled up in bed all day with a book. But she had plans to go shopping with Summer, and as much as she wanted to bail, she knew going would likely make her feel better. The artificial brightness and cheer of the mall—with its too loud upbeat music piping through the concourse and colorful banners, fake skylight, and plastic palm trees—would surely boost her mood. Not to mention, spending time with Summer would keep her out of her own head for a little while.

Despite her decision to go, she still dragged her feet getting ready and was fifteen minutes late by the time she left the house. She jogged the few blocks to Summer's, arriving at the end of her driveway breathless, sweating, and—a quick glance at her watch revealed—twenty minutes late.

Summer stepped out onto the porch before Raven made it even halfway to the house, so she leaned against the side of Summer's car and caught her breath, letting Summer come to her.

"What happened? You get lost?"

Raven just rolled her eyes and circled around the back of the car to slide into the passenger seat.

"Hey, you okay?"

Raven glanced over to find Summer staring at her, brow furrowed in concern. "Yeah, fine. Just tired." She struggled to hold Summer's gaze and to not flinch at the scrutiny she saw in her eyes. The silence in the car had grown to almost uncomfortable levels when Summer turned her attention to starting the car. The radio came on when the engine sprang to life. Raven leaned forward to fiddle with the dials as Summer backed out of the driveway.

"Are you sure you're just tired? Because you're acting weird."

Raven's hand froze on the dial. "Weird how?" she managed, as her mind raced over their interactions for the past few weeks. She fought to pinpoint what Summer might have picked up on and how she would explain herself.

"I don't know. Just weird."

She didn't know whether to be relieved that Summer couldn't identify what was bothering her about Raven's behavior or concerned that she'd keep trying to figure it out.

"I don't know what you're talking about," she said flatly, hoping it would put an end to the conversation. "But, for the last time, I'm fine."

Summer gave her another searching look, then gave a shrug. "All right, then can you please just pick a station and stick to it? All your flipping is driving me nuts."

Raven let out a laugh and sped through a couple more channels before settling on one.

"So, you'll never guess what happened," Summer said.

"What?"

"Jake Martin asked me out tonight. He wants to take me to dinner and then to Noah's party."

"Jake?" He was on the baseball team with AJ and Noah. The pitcher, she believed. He was a grade below them but taking some of their classes. Apparently, he was super smart and would be graduating early. "I didn't know you liked him."

"I didn't. Don't. Not particularly. But he asked me. And, well...he is kind of cute."

"If you say so," Raven said slowly. "When did this happen?"

"I ran into him last night at the park. He was there with his little brother. I was babysitting for the neighbors and the kids wanted to go sledding. We got to talking while the kids played."

"That's great, Summer," she said, trying to match Summer's enthusiasm. She was happy for her, but at the same time, she was also disappointed. They'd been planning on going to this party together as two of the few singles within their group of friends. Now she was going to have to go alone and third wheel herself to the couples there.

"Now we just need to get you hooked up."

"What? Summer, no." She should have seen this coming, should have prepared herself for this inevitable conversation, but she hadn't.

"You know, Greg Barrett was asking about you the other day," Summer continued as if she hadn't spoken. "He's cute, in that nerdy, hipster way."

"I don't want to go out with Greg," she said plainly, hoping it would be enough even though she knew it would not be.

"Why not?"

Because I'm gay.

Because I'm already seeing someone.

The reasons were there on the tip of her tongue, but she couldn't use any of them. She just couldn't say it. Instead, she had to search her mind for an excuse she could actually utter. However, nothing came to her, so she just shrugged.

"Come on. What's wrong with Greg?"

"Nothing."

"Then why won't you go out with him?"

"Because I'm not into him."

"Well, how do you know you couldn't be into him unless you give him a chance?"

Again, the truth was there, but she couldn't bring herself to admit it, even though it would end this conversation and any conversation like it. She just couldn't bear the thought of telling Summer, couldn't bear the possibility of having her oldest friend turn her back on her.

"I don't have to go out with him to know we have nothing in common," Raven answered. "He was on student council with me last year. All he talked about was video games and sci-fi movies. He speaks Klingon. And Navi."

"Navi?" She mouthed the word with a grimace and a shake of her head, but Raven knew the conversation was not over yet. While Summer might be willing to concede that Greg wasn't a match for her, she wasn't going to give up until she got Raven to agree to someone. She hated it when Summer got like this. Whenever she got asked out on a date, it suddenly became her mission to set Raven up with someone as well.

Even though she'd never actually been interested in any of the guys Summer suggested, she'd always eventually given in just to get her off her back. That wasn't an option this time though. She couldn't do that to Morgan. Somehow she was going to have to get Summer to simply drop the subject.

"What about Gabe Denton? He's a sweetheart. And you said you had fun working with him on the winter dance."

"Isn't he all hung up on Kendall Geiger?"

"Okay. Well, how about Charlie? What's his name...from civics last year?"

"You can't even remember his last name. Or the fact that he's in our homeroom this semester, but you think he'd be a good match for me?"

Summer shrugged. "Okay, so it was weak, but at least I'm making an effort."

"But I'm not asking you to."

Summer huffed out a sigh and fell silent. Raven wasn't sure if she'd dropped the subject or if she was just reorganizing her arguments, but she was grateful for the reprieve. Even if the silence that fell between them as they pulled into the mall parking lot was tense and awkward.

"So, any idea what you're getting Noah for his birthday?" Raven asked into the silence.

Summer didn't answer for a long moment, long enough for Raven to wonder if Summer was mad at her.

Finally, Summer shrugged. "Not a clue. You?" Her tone was flat, even, and Raven couldn't tell if she was angry or not.

"Nope."

"Well, it's a good thing we're both so prepared isn't it?" Summer said with a grin.

Raven grinned back, relief washing over her. She'd survived the matchmaking attempts with her secret—and Summer's mood—intact.

CHAPTER TWENTY

Shopping with Summer had been fun but exhausting. They'd walked from one end of the mall to the other, going into nearly every store in search of the perfect gift for Noah, before realizing they had no idea what he might actually want and getting him gift cards.

She was in the middle of putting away her purchases— she'd had a much easier time finding things for herself than she had for Noah—when her cell phone rang, a muted tone from inside her pocket. She fished it out of her jeans. A quick look at the caller ID brought a smile to her face.

"Hey, Morgan."

"You'll never guess what happened," Morgan said by way of greeting, her words a rapid, excited rush.

She cast her bags aside, her full attention on Morgan. "What?"

"You know that art show I was telling you about?"

Raven cast around in her memory, and after a moment, recalled Morgan telling her about the exhibit, a collection of pieces done by students and a few local artists. It was something the gallery did every year. It was rather prestigious and the qualifications for entry were demanding.

"Yeah?" She had a pretty good idea where this was going but was content to let Morgan have her big reveal.

"They've asked me to submit two pieces." She could practically hear the grin in Morgan's voice.

"Two? That's amazing." She knew how much this meant to Morgan. "That's…amazing," she repeated, because it was all she could come up with.

"I know. I'm just…" Morgan's sentence faltered, but Raven knew what she meant.

"I'm so proud of you. I wish I were there right now so I could give you a hug and a kiss," she said, aware of the fact that she was repeating what Morgan had said to her just a few days ago. But this was the kind of news that made her want to just throw her arms around Morgan and squeeze her tight.

"I wish you were, too."

"We have to celebrate. I can be there by—"

"Raven. Rae."

"Yeah?"

"That sounds great. But you've got your party."

"I can skip—"

"*And*…I already have plans with Jules and a few others. We're going to go to that movie thing I told you about."

"Oh." Raven deflated.

"I guess it will have to wait until Wednesday when I come up," she said "And I'll set aside all of next weekend for you." Although it was a reasonable compromise, it left her dissatisfied.

"The whole weekend?" Morgan asked, a gentle tease entering her voice. "What makes you think I'd even want to spend that much time with you?"

Raven scoffed, but a witty response escaped her.

Chapter Twenty-one

The party was in full swing by the time Raven reached Noah's house. Cars lined the street and sat bumper to bumper in the driveway. She was glad she'd walked and wouldn't have to worry about getting blocked in by the time she was ready to leave. Every light inside was on, and music poured out of the basement windows before she'd made it even halfway up the walkway. When she reached the porch, she rang the bell and waited, but nobody came. After a moment's hesitation, she reached for the doorknob. Noah had mentioned at lunch the other day that his parents would be gone for most of the evening, and with everyone gathered downstairs, she doubted anyone had heard her arrival. She felt a little weird letting herself into his house, but it was preferable to standing outside waiting for someone else to come along or a guest inside to come upstairs and spot her.

The music was even louder as she stepped inside, and after kicking off her shoes into the pile by the front door, she followed the sound.

"Raven, hey." Noah was standing near the foot of the stairs as she descended, a red plastic cup in one hand, a couple of darts in the other. He gave her an awkward hug, pulling her close with his forearm as he tried not to spill his drink or poke her with the dart points.

"Happy birthday, Noah." She returned the hug with more ease.

"Glad you could make it. Drinks and stuff are over there. I think there's still some pizza left," he said with a vague wave of his arm to the far corner of the room. The drink in his cup sloshed perilously close to the edge. "And presents are being stacked over there." He gestured in the opposite direction with a smirk and a wiggle of his eyebrows.

Raven made a show of looking down at her empty hands and gave him an apologetic shrug before stepping away and reaching into her purse for the envelope with his gift card in it. She tossed it onto the table and turned, catching his eye and offering a little smirk of her own. He grinned, shook his head, and went back to his game of darts.

She took a moment to survey the room. She spotted Summer and Jake in the corner by the stereo, talking quietly by one of the speakers, and couldn't help but smile at how wrapped up in each other they appeared to be. She didn't notice AJ or Chloe anywhere, so she headed toward the foosball table to say hello to everyone gathered there and maybe get in a game or two.

Two hours later, she was hot and sweaty and breathless but having a great time. She couldn't remember why she hadn't wanted to come. She'd beaten three guys at foosball before AJ stepped in to kick her butt—not all that surprising since he was the one who'd taught her how to play—and had spent the last half hour dancing in the middle of the rec room with Summer and Jake and a few others. The fact that she was single and the majority of the people in the crowd were coupled up didn't even matter. Everyone was mingling and chatting as a group. She didn't feel excluded or intrusive.

"I need something to drink. And to sit down," she yelled into Summer's ear, knowing her words would come out as a dull whisper over the music.

Summer nodded and Raven slipped away, maneuvering her way off the "dance floor" and over to the drinks table. She grabbed a can of soda and headed for the nearest available soft place to sit—an empty couch cushion. She flopped down and took a long pull from her soda. A moment later, the couch dipped beside her.

"Hey, Raven," Jeremy Trent said, giving her an easy smile.

"Jeremy. Hey. Long-time no see," she teased him. He'd been hanging around the foosball table when she'd first arrived. He was one of the guys she'd bested and then they'd chatted for a while after AJ had taken over. He'd also been among the group of dancers who had taken up space in the middle of the living room.

"Yeah, definitely," he said, chuckling lightly.

"Having a good time?" she asked after taking a long pull of soda and then holding the chilled can to her forehead.

"Yeah," he said, nodding slightly. "You looked really good out there." He nodded in the direction of the other dancers.

She wanted to tell him that he'd managed to do a good job of keeping up, but she couldn't. At least not without lying. He'd looked ridiculous, flailing around out there, and she wasn't sure she could return the compliment with a straight face. "My parents will be pleased to know all the money they poured into dance lessons didn't completely go to waste," she said instead.

"Dance lessons?"

"Yeah. Ballet. Nothing like I was doing out there, actually."

"Ballet?" Jeremy shook his head, laughing. "Like, in a tutu?"

"No. No tutus." She decided not to describe the leotards they had worn or the costumes for some of the recitals. She had a feeling he'd find it even more amusing than a tutu.

"Do you still dance?"

"No. I quit years ago."

"Why's that?"

"I was never really that into it. The only reason I even joined was because Chloe did." She glanced toward Chloe, who was dancing in the center of the room with AJ. "When she quit, I quit."

Jeremy nodded. "It was the same thing with me for soccer. My older brother played so I wanted to play. When he got bored of it, so did I."

"So, it wasn't because you sucked?"

"What? No. I was an awesome soccer player."

"Oh. Well, I was a horrible ballerina. I was so glad when Chloe quit and I didn't have to do it anymore."

"No way. I don't believe it."

"Oh, believe it. Go ask Chloe. She'll confirm."

"No, never mind. I'll take your word for it. You ready to get back out there?"

Raven glanced over at the growing crowd of bodies in the center of the room and shook her head.

"Not just yet. I'm beat."

Jeremy nodded and Raven thought he was going to get up, but he merely shifted position so he was half-facing her, his arm stretched out along the back of the couch between them, and started up a conversation about the reading list they had for English class.

Raven had only intended to take a few minutes to catch her breath, have a drink, and cool off, but a few minutes blended seamlessly into thirty minutes, which became sixty minutes, and the next thing she knew the party was winding down and she realized she'd spent half the night on the couch, talking with Jeremy.

"This was fun," he said. "We haven't really had a chance to talk before. It was nice."

She nodded, recognizing the truth in his words. They had spent a lot of time on the periphery of each other's social circles with a number of friends in common and a fair amount of time spent together without ever really spending any time together, just the two of them.

"Yeah," she agreed. "I'm glad we ran into each other." She'd never noticed before how funny he was, her sides hurt from laughing so hard, nor how insightful he was. She'd really enjoyed their conversation.

"We should do this again sometime," he said. "Soon."

"I'd like that."

The next thing she knew, his lips were brushing against hers. Somehow, she'd missed the fact that he'd been shifting closer until his breath was there, hot against her lips. She hadn't really registered when his arm slid from the back of her couch to around her shoulder until he was using it to pull her toward him. Somehow, stupidly, she hadn't seen this coming.

For a moment, she simply sat there, stunned. Then, awareness began to set in, and all she could think was that the kiss was soft and warm and not unpleasant and how much easier it would be if she just gave in to this.

No more secrets.

No more feeling uncomfortable in her own skin.

She would be able to hold his hand in public without feeling self-conscious. She could bring him home to meet her parents and invite him out with her friends.

He increased the pressure, leaning closer, and instead of butterflies, she felt...nothing. Instead of wanting to wrap her arms around him and pull him closer, she had her hands on his shoulders keeping him at a distance, pushing him away. Because even though it might be *easier* to be with Jeremy, she knew she'd never be *happy* with him. Not after having a taste of how it could be, how it *should* be, with Morgan.

Morgan. A flash of panic hit her as she realized what she'd just done.

"Raven?" Jeremy's voice pulled her out of her thoughts. She dragged her gaze to his and saw the questions and confusion there.

She blinked once, twice, trying to clear her head. "I'm sorry, Jeremy, that shouldn't have happened."

He stared at her, brow furrowed in confusion. "We were having a good time. I thought—"

"You weren't wrong, okay? I enjoyed talking with you tonight, but that's all it was, talking."

His confusion faded as his face hardened into a frown.

She reached out to lay a hand on his arm, imploring him to understand and then thought better of it and pulled back. "I'm sorry if I gave you the wrong impression."

Her words fell on deaf ears though. He shook his head, stood up, and walked away without another word. Raven knew she should be more concerned, but as bad as she felt about rejecting Jeremy, her focus was on someone much more important. How could she have done this to Morgan? She might not have initiated the kiss, but she had certainly let it go on long enough before pushing him away. What kind of person did that?

"So, you and Jeremy, huh?" Summer dropped onto the couch beside her. "He's a cutie."

She turned to Summer, staring dumbly at her for a moment before shaking her head. "No. Not me and Jeremy."

"I just saw you kissing him."

She shook her head, not quite sure how to explain.

Summer's teasing grin faded.

"No, it's not his fault. A miscommunication. We'd been talking for a while. I guess he thought it meant more than it did."

"So, you spent like half the night sitting here with him, looking to all the world like you were having a great time, but when he kisses you, you push him away?" Chloe asked, approaching with AJ in tow.

Raven nodded, realizing for the first time that she'd been giving him signals she hadn't meant to give.

"God, Rae, what is going on with you?"

She shrugged, not even knowing where to begin. It was all so tangled that she couldn't explain some without divulging all.

"It's getting late. I'm tired. I'm going to head home," she said, pushing herself up.

Summer and Chloe exchanged glances but thankfully, neither of them decided to push the issue.

CHAPTER TWENTY-TWO

The wind had picked up at some point over the course of the evening. It howled and whipped snow around, forming oddly shaped drifts that tangled around Raven's ankles as she trudged slowly home. If she had been paying attention, she probably would have found the wind biting, but her focus was on the cell phone in her hand and the phone call she knew she had to make.

It wasn't even an option to not tell Morgan. Despite the fact that it had been one kiss and it meant nothing. Even though she hadn't started it, nor had she returned it, and had pushed him away the moment she'd come to her senses. None of that was the point. There were enough secrets in her life right now; she couldn't keep another one. As she listened to the phone ring on the other end, she found herself wishing for the first time since they'd met that Morgan wouldn't answer her phone.

"Hey, Raven." Morgan's voice was warm and cheerful and it only made the knot in her stomach clench tighter.

"Hi."

"You're home early. How was the party?"

"It was good. I had fun. How was your movie night?" Raven was stalling and she knew it.

"It was a lot of fun. They played eighties classics, which you know are my favorite."

Raven nodded. "Yeah. Sounds great. I'm sorry I missed it."

"Next time. They're doing another one in a few weeks."

"I'm there. What are you up to now?" She imagined Morgan lying on her bed in her dorm room, holding the phone up to her ear. Maybe a book in her lap, maybe the remote in hand.

"We're just at the coffee shop."

"You're still with everybody?" Raven asked, feeling a tightening in her chest.

"Yeah."

"Are they like, right there?"

"No. I got up when I saw it was you. I'm standing by the door. Attracting a lot of weird looks right now, just so you know," Morgan said, an edge creeping into her voice. "And when I get back to the table, there are going to be questions."

"What are you going to tell them?"

"I don't know," Morgan said with a sigh. "Is there a reason you called?"

This was not the way this conversation was supposed to start. Raven didn't want to get into this now, but she couldn't exactly back out.

"Something happened at the party tonight."

"Oh?" The question was cautious, but not alarmed.

"There was this guy, Jeremy…" She trailed off for a moment, gathering her courage before finishing off in a rush, "He kissed me."

Silence on the other end of the line.

Raven held her breath waiting for a response, a reaction. "It meant nothing," she said to fill the silence when nothing was forthcoming. "And I didn't kiss him back," she hastened to add. "Please say something."

"What would you like me to say?"

"I don't know, something."

"Give me a minute, okay? I'm still processing." There was a heavy sigh and then more silence. "So, you kissed a guy?"

"*He* kissed *me*. I didn't even see it coming. And I pulled away and told him he'd gotten the wrong idea." Raven paused. "Are you mad?"

"I don't know what I am," Morgan said after a long silence. "You say he came on to you, so I can't really fault you for that. But I hate the thought that I've got to worry about guys hitting on you."

"It was just one guy. At one party."

"But what about the next guy, at the next party? Or the one who sits next to you in class? Or the guy who is a friend of a friend and wants to get to know you better? Guys are going to come on to you. They're going to hit on you and ask you out because you're not giving them any reason not to."

"What's that supposed to mean?"

"What do you think it means, Raven? Yeah, he kissed you. But did you even stop and think about why? About what possible signals you might have been giving him?"

"There were no signals."

"No? So he just, what, walked up to you and kissed you? Out of the blue?"

"No. We were talking and—"

"And you probably spent most of the night with him too, right? Talking, laughing, giving him absolutely no indication that you were with somebody."

"It's not like I could tell him the truth."

"Of course not."

"You *are* mad, but not about the kiss. You're mad because I'm not ready to come out yet."

"So I'm mad. Can you blame me? I'm on the phone in the corner of a coffee shop talking to my *girlfriend*—not for privacy, but because I can't even tell my friends I'm in a relationship. And my girlfriend's telling me she kissed someone else. The fact that it was a guy is irrelevant, Raven. When you're with someone, you don't just go around kissing other people."

"I know that."

"How can you possibly say that, considering what happened tonight? Do you even get how much this conversation hurts right now?"

"Morgan, I—"

"*You* wanted this. *You* pushed for us to be together."

"You make it sound like you didn't want any part of it."

"Don't. You know I have feelings for you. But I can't do this if you're only half-in."

"I'm in this. I swear."

"Then maybe you need to take some time and think about why you're happy to let the rest of the world think you're single. And you're straight."

"Morgan—"

"I can't do this right now, Raven. My friends are waiting for me."

CHAPTER TWENTY-THREE

Raven sat on a bench just off the walkway that linked the path from the dorms to the academic buildings, hunched against the cold, hat pulled down, hands tucked into her pockets, the soup she'd picked up from the deli section of the grocery store on her lap, warming her thighs. She was nervously waiting for Morgan to appear. They hadn't spoken since their fight the night before, and Raven couldn't take it anymore. She'd begged off plans with her friends and had driven up to campus.

She spotted Morgan before Morgan noticed her. She was walking alone, her head bent toward the cell phone in her hands, her thumbs rapidly texting. Raven couldn't tear her eyes away, she was so mesmerized by the sight. Her nerves over a possible continuation of their fight were overridden by the familiar wave and affection she felt every time she laid eyes on Morgan.

A smile tugged at the corners of her lips as she realized Morgan, intent on her texting, was about to walk right past her. Raven jumped, landing almost right in front of her. Morgan let out a yelp of surprise as she pulled to a stop.

"Raven. What are you doing here?" She hesitated a moment and then pulled Raven in for a hug.

Raven melted into Morgan's arms.

"We need to talk about last night. I thought maybe we could have dinner and talk." She raised her arm, drawing Morgan's attention to the grocery bag hanging off her wrist.

"Let's go to my room then," she said and started down the path again. Raven fell into step beside her and the two of them crossed campus in silence.

Morgan unlocked her door and ushered Raven inside ahead of her. The size of the room wasn't so shocking this time, but she still couldn't help but wonder how Morgan could stand to live in such a small space.

"I'm sorry for hanging up on you last night," Morgan said as she sat on the bed, settling cross-legged against the headboard. "And for ignoring all your texts. I was upset, but it was unfair of me to leave you hanging."

Raven nodded, accepting the apology. Being hung up on definitely stung, and it hurt, being ignored all day, but she didn't fault Morgan for her reaction.

"I'm sorry for last night," she said as she slid onto the bed opposite Morgan and placed the bag of soup and sandwiches between them. "I never meant to hurt you."

"I know. But do you get *why* what you did hurt so much?" Morgan asked. "I know things are rough right now," she continued before Raven could respond. "I remember what it was like, coming to terms with being gay, coming out. It's hard and it's scary. But you can't go around kissing guys whenever you feel confused or insecure or—"

"I know. It was a one-time thing, okay? A momentary lapse in judgment."

Morgan took a deep breath, her eyes closing for a brief moment, then she brought her gaze back up to meet Raven's. "Sorry. My last girlfriend cheated on me. It's sort of a sore subject."

Hearing that made Raven feel even worse about what she'd done.

"But it doesn't change the fact that we can't keep going on like this."

Raven was pretty sure she stopped breathing at the words. "What…what do you mean?"

"It means, I can't take much more of this secret relationship. I know things are hard and confusing for you right now. And I'll always care about and support you. But I'm out, Raven. And I won't go back in the closet for you."

"I'm not asking you to."

"Yes, you are. Every time I have to lie to my friends about where I'm going. Every time I have to hug you in public, instead of kissing you like I want to. Every time we walk across campus and I don't take your hand. All the time we spend holed up in here instead of going out, like a normal couple, that's me taking a step backward."

Raven hadn't thought of it like that. "I'm sorry."

"I know. But sometimes sorry isn't enough, Rae."

Raven nodded. It hurt to know her actions were causing Morgan pain.

"I'll work on it, okay? I'll come out to my family, soon. I promise. And in the meantime, let me take you out," she said. "A real date. Somewhere fancy to celebrate your art show. We can get all dressed up and…and it'll be great." She wasn't ready to come out to her family and friends yet, but she could do this for Morgan, could take her out on a proper date. "What do you say?"

"I say it sounds amazing," Morgan said, a grin turning up the corners of her lips as she shifted onto her knees and reached out, her hand snagging Raven's shirt. "Now, come here." She pulled Raven forward. "Know the best part about fighting?" she whispered. "Making up," she finished, before capturing Raven's lips in a kiss.

CHAPTER TWENTY-FOUR

Raven had never planned a date before, and she was nervous. She wanted it to be special, to be perfect, but there were so many things that could go wrong. What if Morgan didn't like the food at the restaurant? Or the waiter was rude? Or the atmosphere was wrong? And she had no idea if she was supposed to bring flowers or hold open doors or pull out chairs.

She was anxious and eager and grateful her parents had left late that morning for lunch and a show with some friends because she knew they would pick up on her distraction. She tried watching movies and reading and doing homework but couldn't stay focused on any one thing for very long. It was a relief when five o'clock rolled around and she had to start getting ready.

She showered, washing and conditioning her hair and then blew it dry before carefully curling it into loose, soft waves that settled around her shoulders. She meticulously applied her makeup, dark browns and smoky grays to draw out her eyes, concealer, blush on her cheeks, a faint sheen on her lips. Her hand remained steady despite the butterflies in her stomach.

She'd picked her dress out days ago, a simple purple baby doll, which she would pair with some ankle boots and a cream cardigan sweater. It would be a little cold, but she had her long, black wool coat, and they would be inside most of the evening.

By just after six, she was ready. She gathered her cell phone, her purse, and the bouquet of lilies she'd picked up after school on Friday and hidden in the cold storage room in the basement, and headed out the door.

As the miles flew past, bringing her closer to her destination, her nervousness began to dissipate until eventually she was feeling only excitement. This was her first real date! The first one she'd truly wanted to go on. She couldn't wait to see how Morgan looked all dressed up. Couldn't wait to hold her hand and stare across the table at her in some dimly lit restaurant, knowing that when she caught Morgan's eye and smiled it was because she was having a wonderful time. And they would have a wonderful time, she was sure of that. From studying in the library to hanging out in Morgan's dorm room, they'd always had a good time together, and tonight wouldn't be any different.

It seemed ridiculous now that she'd ever been worried. So what if the restaurant sucked or the food was horrible or she spilled her drink all over the table? They would laugh about it and move on. Yes, she wanted tonight to be perfect. But if it wasn't, it wouldn't be the end of the world because they'd be together. She already knew Morgan liked her. It wasn't like she had to impress her.

❖

She reached the university just after seven, confident and steady as she climbed out of her car and started toward Morgan's dorm building. As she approached, she shot off a quick text to let Morgan know she was there. She really wished she could have gone up to Morgan's room. Knocking on her door and presenting her with her flowers was much more romantic than waiting in the lobby, but she wasn't a student so security wouldn't let her past unless she was with a resident of the dorms.

A few minutes later, the elevator doors slid open and Morgan stepped out.

"Hey," she said with a smile. Morgan's answering smile was soft and swift.

"Hey," she said as she came to a stop in front of Raven, her arms sliding easily around her waist. Raven returned the embrace, holding Morgan tightly against her for a moment before releasing her and stepping back. Then she glanced around and shifted nervously, noticing several pairs of curious eyes on them.

"These are for you," she said. She cleared her throat and tried not to feel awkward as she presented Morgan with the bouquet of flowers she'd brought.

Morgan's smile grew wider as she took the flowers and lifted them to her nose. "Thank you, Raven. They're beautiful." She took a quick sniff and then lowered the bouquet so she could tilt her head up and give Raven a light kiss.

Raven's cheeks heated and she struggled to keep her gaze on Morgan and not let it drift over to the small crowd of spectators. She really would rather have done this without an audience.

"Shall we go?" she asked, crooking her elbow for Morgan.

"*Shall?*" Morgan teased her as she took the proffered elbow.

Raven shrugged. It had sounded formal and gallant. She was sure she'd heard it on TV.

They walked in an easy, comfortable silence across the campus back to Raven's car.

"Where are we going?" Morgan asked, once they were buckled in.

"Little Italy. I've heard it's amazing." And pricey, but she wasn't going to point that out. She'd gone online looking for good date restaurants, and that one had gotten the best reviews. She'd never been there herself; it was a little out of the way for any of the other dates she'd been on, so she was trusting the word of random strangers on the Internet. They couldn't all be wrong.

Morgan nodded. "I think Jules has mentioned it. That guy she was seeing last semester, Ryan? I think he took her there."

Raven froze. She hadn't been thinking that other students from the university might take their dates there. What if they ran into Jules? Or someone else they knew? After a moment, she relaxed. Julia wasn't seeing anybody right now, and Raven didn't know anyone else who lived around here. "You do like Italian food, right?" she asked. It had seemed like a safe enough choice. Everyone liked pasta.

"I'm not a picky eater," Morgan said. "But, yes, I do like Italian. And Greek, and Chinese, and Thai. I'm not too fond of Indian food though."

Raven nodded, making a mental note. "I don't like sushi," she said. "Something about the idea of eating slimy, uncooked things…" She let out a shudder, which made Morgan laugh.

"Can't say I blame you, when you put it that way. However, I happen to like sushi."

"Say it isn't so." Raven mock gasped.

"Is that a deal breaker?"

"It might be," Raven said, shaking her head in disapproval and sadness. "It just might be."

"Well, what can I do to make you change your mind?"

Raven glanced over. "If you ever do eat sushi..."

"Yeah?"

"Don't tell me. And make sure you brush your teeth really, really well."

Morgan laughed lightly. "It's a deal."

Raven pulled up in front of the restaurant, and before she had a chance to do it herself, the valet was opening Morgan's door for her, guiding her out and over the curb by the hand before crossing around to Raven's side.

"This place is pretty swanky," Morgan said quietly as Raven joined her on the sidewalk. "Are you sure—"

"I'm sure." Raven took her arm and led her toward the front door. Despite such trappings as the valet and the coat check, or the linen tablecloths, heavy silverware, and the crystal glasses, the restaurant wasn't as expensive as it looked. The prices were reasonable, considering. More than her budget could handle on a regular basis, but one night wouldn't bankrupt her.

They checked their coats, then checked out each other for the first time.

"Wow, you look amazing," Raven breathed, stunned by the full picture of Morgan all dressed up.

Morgan's face lit up in a soft smile. "So do you."

Raven's cheeks heated from Morgan's open, obviously approving appraisal.

The hostess led them to a table along the far wall, fairly secluded by ivy-covered lattices that served as decoration as well as sectioning the dining room off into several smaller areas. There were three other tables in their section and only one was occupied, by an elderly couple lost in their own little world. They hadn't even looked up at Raven and Morgan as the hostess led them through.

"Your menus," said the hostess, laying them on the table. "Your server will be over momentarily."

"Thank you," Raven murmured as she slid into her seat across from Morgan.

The lack of other diners, low lighting, and flickering candle glow created a sense of intimacy that had Raven relaxing into her chair and reaching across the table to take Morgan's hand in her own.

"This place is nice," Morgan said softly as she glanced around. "I like the frescoes on the wall."

"You would notice those," Raven teased her gently. "You're such an art nerd."

The paintings on the wall were quite beautiful though. She could see why they'd caught Morgan's eye, art student or not. The one beside them was an incredibly realistic rendering of the coliseum at night. It felt like they were sitting under the stars in the shadow of the ruins.

Morgan ignored her art nerd comment as she studied the painting. Raven watched her, charmed by the intensity of her focus, taking in the details, or admiring the technique, or whatever it was she was doing. Raven didn't know for sure, and to be honest, she didn't care. She didn't understand art the way Morgan did, but she enjoyed watching her geek out over it.

"You're staring at me," Morgan murmured as she turned back from the painting.

"Yep." Raven didn't bother to hide or deny it. She couldn't help it. Morgan was looking especially pretty tonight. Her dark green dress brought out the flecks in her eyes. She'd swept up her hair into a loose bun at the nape of her neck.

She watched the corners of Morgan's mouth fight off a smile for a moment before Morgan ducked her head, grinning, as her cheeks darkened. "Why don't you stare at your menu?" Morgan mumbled. "And stop being creepy."

Raven laughed and gave Morgan's hand a squeeze but obeyed, picking up her menu with her free hand and giving it a once-over.

"Now who's being creepy?" she asked a moment later. She glanced over the top of her menu and caught Morgan gazing at her. A rush of warmth spread through her entire body at the frank, unabashed stare from Morgan.

CHAPTER TWENTY-FIVE

"This is the most amazing meal I've ever eaten," Morgan said as she dropped her fork onto her plate with a clatter. "But if I eat another bite, I'm going to explode."

"I know what you mean," Raven said, admitting defeat. The spinach ravioli she'd ordered was delicious, but she'd been pushing the last few squares around for a while now, unable to eat anything else despite her attempts to clean her plate. "Too bad though, because I was really looking forward to dessert."

"Yeah. Me, too. Did you see the tiramisu?"

Raven shook her head. "No. But I saw they had zeppole." As much as she wanted something sweet, it would be too much right now. However, maybe if they took a walk they'd find a coffee shop and be ready for some dessert by then. It wasn't that cold tonight, and she wasn't ready for their date to end.

When the check came, she grabbed it quickly, before Morgan could get a peek at the price. She felt Morgan's eyes on her as she opened her wallet, so she schooled her face into a neutral expression, refusing to show any sort of reaction as she glanced at the total and then slid her "emergency" credit card along with the check back to the waiter.

She was going to have to make sure she got to the mail before her parents did because if they saw this charge, they would flip. But despite the worried glances Morgan kept shooting her way, she wasn't concerned about actually paying it off. She'd be back to work again in a few months. And no matter the cost, it was worth it.

The waiter returned with her card and her receipt, which she signed with a flourish. Once they were alone again, she stood and offered Morgan a smile. "Shall we?"

"You're such a dork," Morgan said with a roll of her eyes, but she stood and tucked her arm in the crook of Raven's elbow. "Thank you for dinner. For tonight," Morgan said softly as they made their way back through the restaurant to get their coats.

A burst of pride had Raven standing up a bit straighter. All her stressing over this date had been for nothing. Morgan had liked the restaurant, the food had been good, and nobody had bothered them. She was getting the hang of this date thing… bringing flowers, holding doors. It was fun.

Snow fell lightly when they stepped outside, but the temperature was still mild.

"Still up for a walk?"

Morgan nodded and took her hand, lacing their fingers together before starting down the street. Raven fell into step beside her, using their joined hands to pull Morgan closer until their shoulders were brushing.

The snow fell steadily around them, a soft, shifting curtain that obscured the cars whizzing steadily past and muted the sounds of the shops around them closing up for the night. It created a cozy little world that existed just for the two of them.

"When it snows like this, it makes me want to make snow angels."

"Go right ahead," Raven replied, giving her a nudge in the direction of an undisturbed patch of snow in the alley between a dry cleaner and a deli.

"In this dress? I'd freeze."

"You know I'd keep you warm." Raven extracted her hand from Morgan's grasp and wrapped her arm around Morgan's shoulders, nearly tripping them both as their feet got tangled together.

Morgan laughed lightly. "Seems more like you want to throw me into a snowbank."

Raven let out a gasp. "I would never."

"Uh-huh." Morgan shook her head and gave her a wide berth as they continued down the sidewalk. Raven reached for her only to have her hand batted away. She lunged, catching Morgan around the waist and propelling them forward. Rather than throw Morgan into a snowbank, she guided her into the recessed doorway of a bakery, backing her against the wall and then pressing up against her as she tilted her head to capture Morgan's lips in a kiss.

Morgan's body sagged against hers, and her hands relaxed their grip on her arms, falling away momentarily before coming to rest at the small of her back, bunching up fabric of her jacket as she pulled her in closer.

When they parted, she was breathless. She never knew kissing could feel like this until Morgan, and now she couldn't get enough. A little light-headed, she leaned in once again.

It was Morgan who pulled away the second time. "God, Raven." Her voice hitched on the last syllable as her head dropped down into the crook of Raven's shoulder. She shivered at the sensation of Morgan's breath washing across the skin above the collar of her jacket and felt Morgan chuckle into her neck at the reaction.

"Want to head back?" Morgan suggested. "We could grab some dessert from the cafeteria, go up to my room, and continue this somewhere a little warmer. And without bricks digging into my back."

"Sorry about that." She brushed a soft kiss to Morgan's temple and then stepped back. She took Morgan's hand in her own and guided them both out of their little alcove.

"So, I have a question for you," Morgan said a few minutes later. "You know my art show's coming up."

"Yeah."

"Well, I'd really like it if you'd come."

"You'd really want me there?" she asked, unable and unwilling to do anything about the grin threatening to crack her cheeks.

"Of course I want you there," Morgan said, giving her hand a little tug so their shoulders bumped together. "You're my girlfriend and this is an important night for me."

"I know. And I'd be honored."

"Even though you hate art?"

"I don't *hate* art. I just don't understand it the way you do."

"Good," Morgan said, a grin lighting up her face. "I'm so glad you won't be bored. I just want everyone to have a good time."

"Everyone?"

Morgan nodded. "Yeah. I invited Jules, Cindy, and Liv, and a few others. I sent an invite to my parents, but I know they won't be able to make it."

"Wait—your friends are coming?"

Morgan's grin faded into a frown as she came to a stop, and she tugged Raven around gently to face her. "Yes, my friends are coming. This art show is a big deal, and I want the people I care about to be there."

Raven understood that, she really did. It was just…did Morgan understand what she was asking? Did she grasp how hard it would be for Raven to be there at that art show amongst all of Morgan's friends? She wasn't ready for that. She just couldn't do it.

She opened her mouth, then let it fall shut again when no words came out. Apparently, none were necessary.

Morgan's jaw tightened. "Really, Raven? I mean, we're on a date, in public. We've made progress, or at least I thought so."

"I'm sorry." The words were hoarse, her voice cracking on the last syllable.

"Wow." Morgan huffed out a sigh. "We *just* talked about this," Morgan said. "And I'm not even asking you to come and hold my hand or anything. I'm not going to kiss you in front of everyone. I'm asking you to come, as my *friend*, and you can't even do that for me?

Raven wanted to, but just the thought of it set her heart hammering. They weren't just friends. When she was near Morgan, the desire to be next to her, to touch her, to kiss her was just so strong. She didn't think she would be able to hide it around other people.

Morgan tugged her hand, trying to extract her fingers from Raven's grasp. She tried to tighten her grip and link them back together, but Morgan shook her off and took a step back.

"Morgan, wait. I—"

"No." Morgan held up a hand. "I knew, going in, that you were struggling. But I thought if we took things slowly, you would start to feel more comfortable. And you've come a long way. You have. But I can't be with someone who won't even acknowledge me in public."

Raven had no defense because she knew Morgan was right.

"I need a little more time," Raven said,

"How much longer?" Morgan asked. "A week? A month? A year?"

She opened her mouth to answer and then realized she had none to give.

Tears pricked at the corners of her eyes, and she didn't even attempt to stop them from falling. She let them spill over onto her cheeks. "I'm sorry, Morgan."

Morgan nodded and offered a small, sad smile. "Me too."

The tears fell faster as Morgan made no move to comfort her.

"I'm going to walk back," Morgan said as she shoved her hands deep into her jacket pockets and shifted in place. "It's only a few blocks."

She nodded once, briskly, and wiped at her eyes with the sleeve of her jacket.

With one last sad smile, Morgan turned and started down the block.

Raven stood rooted in place, watching until she rounded the corner.

CHAPTER TWENTY-SIX

The drive home passed in a blur. She kept her eyes focused on the road, refusing to let herself think about what had just happened, but the tears kept pooling in her eyes, obscuring her vision until she managed to blink them away. Somewhere in the back of her head she knew she shouldn't be driving right now, but she just wanted to get home, and get out of this dress that reminded her of Morgan.

By the time she made it, her jaw ached from the tension of holding back sobs. A few more minutes, and she'd be free to let it all out. She parked in the garage and came in through the side entrance, avoiding both the kitchen and the living room to escape upstairs unseen by her parents. Once in her room, she flung herself down onto her bed, face buried in her pillow, and let the tears fall in earnest.

A few minutes later, a knock sounded on the door and she tensed, her breath catching in her throat as she tried to hold back a sob.

"Raven, honey?" It was her mother. "We'd like to talk to you."

"Uh, just a minute," she called out as she wiped hastily at her eyes. "I'm...I'm changing."

She rolled off the bed and shimmied out of her dress, letting it pool on the floor without a single concern of it getting wrinkled or dirty. It's not like she'd ever wear it again. She riffled quickly through her dresser drawer for a pair of sweats and an old T-shirt, pulling them on hastily before tying her hair back into a loose ponytail to hide the curls, and then flopped back down onto her bed.

"Okay, you can come in," she called as she settled against the pillows, drawing her knees up to her chest and wrapping her arms around them.

The door creaked open and her mother's face peeked into view.

"What's wrong?" Raven asked, noticing the furrow in her mom's brow as she stepped fully into the room. Her heart beat faster, pounding in her ears over the ensuing silence. "Guys?" She heard the worried note in her tone as they approached the bed, her mother taking a seat on the edge beside her and her father leaning against the windowsill to her left.

"Nothing's wrong," her mother said softly as she reached out and laid her hand over Raven's. "But we're worried about you. You've been acting different lately, and we were wondering if something's going on."

"I'm fine," she replied automatically.

"You've been distant and distracted lately," her father said. "Clearly, you're not fine."

"Are you having problems at school?"

She glanced over at her mother and then down at the hand on her arm, squeezing tenderly. "School's fine. You saw my midterm grades. They're all good."

"What about the kids at school? Are you…getting along with everyone?"

"I'm not being bullied, Mom." As much as she appreciated their concern, she really did not want to be having this conversation right now.

"You're friends haven't been around much. Are you guys fighting?"

"No."

"Then what's going on?" her father asked.

"Nothing is going on. Nothing's wrong. I'm fine," Raven insisted, tears pricking at the corners of her eyes at the lie. Nothing was fine. She was falling apart. Her world had been turned upside down, and she'd lost the one person who'd made it seem like everything might still be okay. She'd been dumped for the first time, and she couldn't even tell anybody, because nobody knew she'd been in the relationship in the first place.

"You're not pregnant, are you?"

Raven let out a laugh, even though there was nothing remotely funny about the question. She saw her parents exchange a concerned glance and bit her lip, quelling her reaction. "I'm not pregnant," she said firmly.

"Is it...have you gotten involved in drugs?"

"Oh my God, Mom!"

"We've been watching you struggling for the past few weeks," said her dad, "and we can't do it anymore."

"Raven?" She glanced up into her mother's pleading eyes, and she felt some of her resolve break. "Whatever it is, we can help you."

They couldn't.

There was no way they could help her with this.

But she was just so tired. Keeping secrets was exhausting. Maybe it would be all right to tell them. Maybe they wouldn't freak out, wouldn't disown her. Maybe her mom would hold her and tell her everything was going to be all right, and that she'd find somebody else someday. It all seemed too much to hope for, yet within her grasp at the same time. In the end, she told them the only thing she could…

"I'm gay."

CHAPTER TWENTY-SEVEN

The silence that followed was deafening, and Raven wished she could take it back. Because one glance at her parents revealed that it had been the exact wrong thing to say. From the shell-shocked expression and tears in her mother's eyes, to the anger flashing across her father's face, she knew they would rather she were pregnant or addicted to drugs.

Anything but what she actually was.

"Absolutely not," her father said, his voice calm and even, which was worse than when he was angry and yelling.

"I know dating can be difficult, especially at your age," her mom said softly, "but giving up is not the answer."

"What? You think...it's not because I haven't been able to find a boyfriend. I don't like boys."

"You're a late bloomer, like my sister," her mom said. "She didn't date seriously until college."

"Are you even listening to me?" Raven didn't know why she was pushing this. Clearly, they weren't going to accept this, accept her. The best thing to do would be to shut up, agree to whatever excuses they made, and pretend this conversation had never happened. But she couldn't seem to make herself do that. Instead, she found herself sitting there, trying to make her parents understand.

"I don't like boys," she repeated. "I like girls. I'm attracted to girls."

"You've always been a tactile person," her mother said. "And I know how girls are, especially these days, hugging, kissing, holding hands. I can see how you'd confuse affection for attraction. But one day, you'll meet the right guy and you'll see the difference."

"God, Mom. Do you hear yourself? Do you realize how you sound?" She paused for an answer. None came. "I'm not saying I'm gay because I'm lonely and I like how it feels when my friends hold my hand. You wanted to know what's been bothering me the last few weeks. Well, I need you to listen to what I'm telling you." She slid off the bed, unable to be still any longer with all this built-up tension inside her. She shifted uneasily at the foot of the bed, trying to catch her parents' eyes, but neither of them would look directly at her.

"I'm gay. I'm attracted to girls. I like to hug them and hold their hands and kiss them, but it's more than that. It's not just physical." She saw them flinch at her words, but now that she had started, she couldn't stop. "And it freaks me out, too. I denied it. I ignored it. I pretended I felt like all my friends do. But it's just here"—she laid a palm over her chest—"inside me, and I can't do anything about it." She pleaded with them to understand.

Her father's gaze remained stony as he stared at a point somewhere over her shoulder. Her mother fingered the silver cross hanging around her neck as her gaze held steady on the bedspread beneath her.

"We can take you to talk to someone about this. Maybe Dr. Jordin can recommend—"

"A doctor can't fix this, Mom. It's not like when you get the flu. There's no antibiotic that'll take away the gay."

"Don't take that tone with your mother," her father snapped. "We've raised you better than this."

"Better than what? Talking back or being a lesbian?"

He didn't reply.

"Sorry," she muttered. "I'm not saying this to upset you. I never wanted to disappoint you. I tried not to be gay, but it just got to be too much. Morgan said—"

"Morgan?" her father interrupted. "Is she the one who filled your head with such thoughts?"

She winced as she realized what she had just done. She hadn't meant to bring Morgan into this. "You mean did Morgan make me gay? No."

"But she does have something to do with this?"

Reluctantly, Raven nodded. "She's my girlfriend. Was."

"How long? How long have you been seeing this girl?" He sneered the word, as if even saying it was distasteful. "Sneaking around and lying to us?"

When he put it that way, Raven didn't want to tell him. She didn't want to tarnish the brief relationship they'd had by subjecting it to his anger and obvious disgust. And, technically, she had not been lying. Every time she'd gone to see Morgan, she'd told her parents exactly where she was going. She just hadn't mentioned that there would be kissing and cuddling and hand-holding. Somehow, she hadn't thought they'd appreciate those finer points. But she could tell from the hard edge in his voice, now was not the time to be defiant. "A couple of weeks. Just after she started helping me study for my exam."

"You're grounded."

"I'm what?

"Grounded."

"So…what? No phone, no computer, until I'm not a lesbian anymore?" She shook her head. They weren't getting it. They were never going to get it. And she couldn't take any more. She was shivering, so worked up. Angry tears stung her eyes, and she refused to let her parents reduce her to tears. Without another word, she turned and walked out of the room.

Raven wasn't sure whether to be relieved or resentful that neither of her parents tried to stop her from leaving. It's not that she had any desire to continue the conversation, but shouldn't they have made at least a token effort? She listened for the sound of footsteps or a voice calling after her, but all was silent behind her as she pulled on her coat, jammed her feet into her boots, and slipped out of the house.

Ignoring the torrent of tears and the implications of what she had just done, Raven thrust her hands deep into her pockets and started walking. The streets were dark and deserted. Not a single soul, not even one car passed her as she wandered without destination.

She couldn't, wouldn't, allow herself to think about what had happened. She was just taking a walk, enjoying the night air, and the fresh blanket of snow—that's what she kept telling herself as she turned corners when she came to them and crossed intersections on autopilot. Because if she let herself think about the fact that she'd just come out to her parents, and then walked out in the middle of them flipping out, she'd break down on the spot.

She couldn't do that.

She walked until she couldn't walk anymore. Until her feet were numb and her cheeks burned, until she shivered with cold. Even then, she wasn't ready to go home. When she finally took in her surroundings, she found herself about four blocks from home, across the street from the park where she and her friends had played after school when she was younger…and about two blocks from Summer's house.

It wasn't until she'd rung the doorbell that Raven realized Summer was going to want some kind of explanation as to why she was on her doorstep at nearly midnight, but it was too late to change her mind now. She heard the faint thud of footsteps in the hallway, and a moment later, the door swung open to reveal a confused, pajama-clad Summer, blinking at her.

"Raven?" Summer opened the screen door and stepped forward so they were face-to-face.

"I had a fight with my parents," Raven said softly, blinking away the tears that formed as her words conjured up the memory. "Can I stay here tonight?"

Summer's expression transformed from confused to stunned, but she nodded and stepped back, ushering Raven in. "Of course. Yeah. Come in."

"Thanks." She managed a wan smile as she stepped past her.

Summer hovered by her shoulder, waiting as she shed her winter clothes, and then silently led the way upstairs. Raven knew Summer was curious and was grateful she wasn't pressing for details.

When they made it to her room, Summer flopped down on her bed and turned her gaze to Raven, who stood uncertainly on the threshold. Normally, she'd flop down beside Summer, elbows and knees bumping as they jostled for space and not think anything of it, but now she felt hesitant. Summer might not want Raven on the bed with her when she told her what the fight with her parents had been about. She pulled out Summer's desk chair and settled on that.

Summer raised an eyebrow but didn't comment. Instead, she slid forward on the bed and sat cross-legged at the end, studying Raven in silence as she waited.

Raven knew if she told Summer she didn't want to talk about it, Summer would accept that, dying of curiosity or not. And it was tempting, so very tempting to just say nothing, to keep the details of this night to herself and go on as if nothing had changed. But tonight's events—Morgan, her parents, all of it—caused an ache in her chest. Foolish as it may be to think Summer could make it better, Raven had to at least try.

For better or worse, she was going to come out to her best friend.

"There's something I haven't told you," she began, meeting Summer's gaze and then averting her eyes, deciding that if Summer was going to look at her the same way her parents had, she didn't want to see it. "Not because I was keeping secrets, but because I didn't know how to tell you. I didn't know how you'd react."

She glanced up quickly. Summer stared intently at her, brow furrowed, nibbling her bottom lip as she waited. Raven took a deep breath and refocused on her hands, twisting in her lap.

"I'm gay."

A moment of silence ensued, followed by the rustle of covers as Summer slid off the bed. Raven braced herself for whatever came next: anger, yelling, demands to get out. She felt Summer in front of her, but couldn't bring herself to look up. The next thing she knew, Summer had knelt in front of her and put her arms around her shoulders as she drew her into a hug. Raven's entire body sagged with relief, and she melted into the touch, clinging to her as sobs ripped through her body.

Summer rubbed soothing circles across her back and stroked her hair, until her tears subsided and her breathing evened out to just the occasional hiccup. When she pulled back, she didn't go far. She sat back on her heels, one hand on Raven's knee as she reached for a box of tissues with the other.

"Thank you," Raven said when she was able to speak again.

"Of course." Summer gave her leg one last squeeze before rising to her feet and dropping onto the bed, sitting at the end, her feet hanging over the edge so they bumped against Raven's as she swung them lightly.

It wasn't the reaction she had expected, but it was the one she'd been hoping for. At least one thing had gone right tonight. She didn't think she could've handled another rejection. She only hoped Summer was actually as okay with this as she appeared to be, because Raven was going to need someone to talk to. Right now, though, she just wanted to close her eyes and forget that tonight had even happened. Emotional exhaustion took over. "Can we...do you mind if we talk about this more tomorrow?" she asked. "I'm just...I'm so tired."

Summer nodded. "Whatever you need."

"Thank you. Again. For everything." She reached over and squeezed her hand, eyeing her for a reaction, any indication that she was uncomfortable, but Summer didn't even blink. She just squeezed back and offered a soft smile.

After a moment, Raven let their joined hands drop and stood. They got ready for bed in silence, but it was a comfortable silence, one borne of familiarity and routine. It wasn't until they were both settled in when Summer broke the silence, her voice quiet in the darkness that shrouded them.

"Hey, Rae?"

"Yeah?"

"This changes nothing. You're still my best friend. I still love you."

Raven nodded, even though she knew Summer couldn't see.

"And, Raven?"

"Yeah?"

"Thank you for trusting me enough to tell me."

She let out a soft murmur, her throat too thick with tears for words.

CHAPTER TWENTY-EIGHT

The bed was empty when Raven woke the next morning. From the sounds and smells drifting up from downstairs, she assumed Summer was in the kitchen giving her parents an abbreviated version of last night. She knew Summer's parents wouldn't mind that she'd spent the night, and she doubted Summer would reveal her secret without okaying it with her first, but she still didn't feel like going downstairs and facing them. She wasn't up for dealing with people today. All she wanted to do was curl up and wallow. Since her bed wasn't available for wallowing at the moment, Summer's would have to do. She grabbed the remote and aimed it at the TV perched on the corner of the desk. It sprang to life, and she idly flipped channels, not really in the mood for anything but wanting something to distract her from her thoughts.

About twenty minutes later, she heard footsteps on the stairs, then Summer's door creaked open slowly.

"Hey," she said softly, stepping into the room with a tray balanced across one arm.

"Morning."

"So, I realize today is an ice cream and movies kind of day, but it's not quite noon yet, and my mom wouldn't go for me bringing a carton up here, so I had to settle."

As she approached, Raven got a look at the food piled high onto plates, waffles topped with ice cream, whipped cream and fresh cut fruit, and she couldn't help but smile.

"I think it'll do," she said as she balanced the tray while Summer slid onto the bed beside her. "Thank you, Summer." And she meant for more than just the breakfast, although that was definitely part of it.

Summer gave a faint shrug as she settled back against the pillows and pulled one of the plates onto her lap. They ate in silence, an old-school cartoon that brought back memories of childhood flickering across the screen in front of them. It wasn't until their plates had been scraped clean and set aside on the floor that Summer turned to her and asked, "Do you want to talk?"

"No," she said with a sigh. She so desperately wanted to pretend everything from last night hadn't happened. But part of what had occurred had been exactly because she'd spent too much time hiding and denying what was going on. Morgan had broken up with her because she couldn't, or wouldn't, face up to who she was. "But I think I need to."

"You don't have to, but I think you should," Summer agreed.

"I don't even know where to start," she said. There was so much ground to cover.

"Why don't you start with...how long have you known?"

"A while. Longer than I was willing to admit it to myself, anyway." She couldn't pinpoint exactly when the feeling or the inkling of knowledge had begun, but she knew it had been lingering for years. "But I guess I really started to know a few weeks ago."

Summer nodded, following along, and Raven was glad Summer was so accepting. She needed that, someone steady, someone she could lean on right now.

"Right around the time Morgan started helping me study for my art exam."

Summer's eyes widened with surprise. "You have a crush on Morgan?" she asked, her voice going up in pitch at the sheer surprise of it.

Raven bit back a grin, perversely enjoying her shock. "Yeah. I didn't know what it was at first. I couldn't understand why I kept…responding to her the way I was. That first night, I thought it was just me being uncomfortable around her because she was gay and I'd never met anyone who was before."

"You freaked out and ran into the bathroom," Summer said slowly. "That was because—"

"I was imaging what it would be like to kiss Morgan, and there she was next to me, like right next to me, my whole body was buzzing from her touch."

"And then, back up in my room you—I accused you of being a homophobe. Oh, Rae, I'm so sorry."

"It's fine, Summer. What else were you to think? I was so confused; it's not like I could tell you what was really going on in my head."

Summer nodded, mollified by her words, and Raven continued, explaining how they'd gotten close over the course of studying, and how it started getting harder for her to deny what was really going on. "And so I kissed her. Then I flipped out and took off."

"Wait a minute—you kissed Morgan?" Summer asked, sounding incredulous, and Raven was ashamed to admit she was actually enjoying this. Just a little. She'd never gotten to have this kind of talk with her friends before, the slow reveal of attraction and retelling of events that led to that first kiss, that first date.

"Yes, I kissed Morgan." She took a deep breath and braced herself for the big reveal. "More than once, actually. We were kind of…we were…dating."

Summer's eyebrows shot up toward her hairline. "Come again? You and Morgan are—you have a girlfriend?"

The question brought tears to her eyes, and she blinked away their sting. She'd been doing all right so far, not getting emotional about it, not really letting herself think about what it was she was saying, but hearing that word brought it all back. It reminded her this wasn't just a story she was telling, and it was more than teasing Summer with the slow parceling out of information. She'd gotten her heart broken the night before, and it was all her own fault.

At the sight of her tears, Summer wrapped her arm around Raven's shoulders and pulled her in tight. "I'm not judging you or anything. I'm just surprised. I wasn't expecting that."

Raven wiped her eyes. "I know. It's okay," she said. "That's not what's upsetting me. Morgan and I broke up last night."

"Oh, Rae." Summer's one-arm embrace became a full hug. Raven relaxed into her arms, resting her head against Summer's shoulder, as the whole tale came spilling out.

"They wouldn't even look at me," she said quietly when she got to the confrontation with her parents. "My dad was pissed. And my mom kept telling me it was just because I was lonely and hadn't met the right guy. They wanted me to go talk to someone, as if that would fix me or something."

Summer squeezed her sympathetically but didn't say anything. What was there to say, really?

"I don't know how I'm going to face them again," Raven said, thinking of how awkward and horrible it was going to be when she finally had to go home. She couldn't stay camped out on Summer's bed forever.

"Maybe they just need a chance to process what you told them," Summer said softly. "It's a lot to take in."

"Are you taking their side in this?" Raven pulled away so she could turn and look at Summer, who was shaking her head and reaching out to draw Raven back in.

"Of course not. It's horrible, the stuff they said to you. I'm just saying, you sort of dropped a bomb on them and expected them to just be automatically okay with it." Summer slid her arm across Raven's shoulder and squeezed her lightly. "Were you okay with it, when you first realized you were gay?"

"God, no. I was so freaked out..." Raven trailed off, understanding the point Summer was trying to make.

"Look, I know it sucks. And it hurts because they're your parents. But you've had a couple of weeks to get used to the idea. Give them the same chance. Let them cool down a little and then try and talk to them again."

Raven nodded, reluctantly admitting what Summer said made sense. After a few minutes, her words even started to give Raven hope. Maybe after having the chance to process, they were regretting their reactions. Maybe now, they wouldn't be so narrow-minded.

CHAPTER TWENTY-NINE

"What are you doing there, Rae? Looking for Narnia?" She jumped at the sound of Summer's voice behind her, and a blush heated up her cheeks as she realized she'd been standing in front of the closet staring into it since she'd stepped out of the bathroom from her shower. She gripped the towel wrapped around her so it wouldn't slip, and turned. "Just because you've never found it, doesn't mean it doesn't exist." She grabbed a T-shirt and jeans and ducked just inside the bathroom to dress.

Summer just rolled her eyes and glanced down at her phone, which had pinged a new text coming in. "It's Chloe," she said. "She wants to know if I'm up for coffee or something, this afternoon. And if I know where you are. She's texted you a bunch of times, apparently."

Chloe.

Raven froze in mid-step. Chloe had no idea what had happened last night, what had been going on for the last few weeks. She liked the idea of being able to talk openly with Summer about what she was going through, and she didn't want to worry about weighing her words or censoring herself when Chloe was around. She was just so tired of it, of trying to figure out what was safe to say, and to whom. "Can you tell her I'm here and that my phone died, or something?" She'd left it behind on her rush out the door last night. "And maybe that you can't, but I'd like to meet up for coffee?"

Summer glanced up from her phone and gave her a searching look. "Are you sure?"

Raven nodded, despite the butterflies that erupted in her stomach at the thought.

"You know she might not take it well."

Raven considered that. She'd been considering it for weeks now. It was part of what had made her so reluctant to tell anyone in the first place, but there was also the possibility Chloe would be as lovely and supportive as Summer was being. She had to know. "I know."

"And you really don't want me to go with you?"

"I do, actually," she admitted. "But I think it's something I need to do by myself. I don't want Chloe to feel like we're ganging up on her or something."

"Are you coming back here when you're done?"

Raven shrugged. "Depends on how it goes, I guess." If Chloe flipped out, Raven was definitely going to need Summers's shoulder to cry on. If she took it well, that might be the boost she needed to go home and face her parents.

Summer nodded. "Call me if you need me."

Before Raven could remind her that she was without her cell phone, Summer tossed hers to Raven across the room.

"You really don't have to—"

"Call me," Summer interrupted her. "And I'll come get you."

Raven nodded and tucked the phone into her jean pocket. "I love you; you know that?"

Summer grinned. "Of course you do. I'm awesome."

It was lame, but it made Raven smile as she turned and headed downstairs.

CHAPTER THIRTY

Had she been driving, it would have taken Raven about two minutes to get to their favorite coffee shop downtown. Walking, it took closer to twenty, but she still arrived before Chloe. She ordered a latte and a brownie and took a seat in the back corner where she could watch the flames in the fake fireplace flicker while she waited.

She tried not to over think the conversation ahead of her, worried she'd get nervous and end up stumbling and stuttering over her words. Instead, she kept her mind deliberately blank as she nibbled on her brownie. She had just popped the last bite into her mouth when she spotted Chloe stepping through the door, scanning the crowd. She offered a small wave, then went back to watching the flames while Chloe went to the counter to order.

A few minutes later, the scent of cinnamon preceded Chloe to the table. Raven looked up just in time to see her slide into the chair across from her, a mug in one hand, a cinnamon bun on a plate in the other.

She smiled a greeting, but it felt—and no doubt looked—forced.

"Hey. You all right? You look beat."

The nerves she had been avoiding hit Raven, and suddenly, it was hard to breathe. Raven put her coffee down and forced herself to meet Chloe's gaze. "There's something I need to tell you," she began slowly, recycling the words from last night because she didn't know how else to ease herself into it. "Not because I wanted to keep things from you but because I just didn't know how to tell you."

"Hey, you know you can tell me anything," Chloe said, reaching out and giving Raven's arm an encouraging squeeze.

Raven stared down at the spot where Chloe's hand rested against her skin and hoped that was true. Her heart hammered in her ears. She licked her lips, took a deep breath, and braced for whatever came next. "I'm gay." The confession passed her lips as little more than a quiet gasp of air, and she watched Chloe's face carefully, waiting for her reaction.

For a long moment, Chloe remained utterly still, her expression blank, and then her eyes widened, almost comically so. "You're gay?"

Raven nodded.

"Oh. Okay." Chloe let out a sort of sigh and shifted in her chair, her hand slipping off Raven's arm as she sat back. A heavy silence descended as they sat there, Chloe staring down at the table as if it were the most interesting thing in the room, and Raven staring at her.

"Chloe? Say something. Please."

"I don't know what you want me to say."

"Just tell me you don't hate me."

Chloe's head shot up at that, and she met Raven's eyes. "I don't hate you. I could never hate you. It's just, weird, you know? I've always thought it was…not wrong, really, but not

right either. Two girls together? Two guys? It's just kind of..."
Chloe ran a hand through her curls. "But you're my best friend
and..." She trailed off again and shrugged as her gaze shifted
back down to the table for a moment, before returning to meet
Raven's. "You're my best friend," she repeated. "I don't want
to lose you. So, I'll try, okay?"

An uncomfortable silence settled over the table as they
sat sipping their coffees and looking everywhere but at each
other. Raven's eyes roamed the room as she wracked her brain
for something to say. She hated this tongue-tied feeling around
Chloe, and she was glad when she finished the last few sips of
her drink. "Well, I guess I should be going," she said softly,
pushing her mug across the table idly.

Chloe nodded. "Yeah. Me, too."

They both stood and gathered their things and headed for
the front door.

"I'm parked around back." Chloe jerked her thumb in
the general direction of the lot behind the building as soon as
they'd cleared the front door. She didn't bother to ask where
Raven was parked or if she needed a ride. Raven didn't ask
for one.

"I'll see you at school then?" Chloe asked, taking small,
shuffling backward steps even as she spoke.

"Yeah. See you tomorrow."

Chloe nodded and offered a small wave before turning
and striding away.

Raven watched her go, waiting until she'd rounded the
corner before shoving her hands into her pockets and heading
off in the opposite direction. It hadn't been the most enthusiastic
of acceptances. While she was grateful Chloe hadn't freaked

out or taken off, she couldn't help but think that a true friend wouldn't have to *make an effort* to be her friend. She wouldn't have to *try* not to treat her differently, or not feel awkward around her. This one piece of information shouldn't affect a decade of friendship.

Except it did.

Chapter Thirty-one

There were no cars in the driveway, but a couple of the lights were on downstairs, so Raven knew somebody was home. She made her way slowly up the walkway, and after a moment's pause on the front steps, let herself into the house. The entryway and living room were dark, but light spilled out into the hallway from the kitchen, as did the faintest strains of music, and Raven gravitated toward both.

When she reached the doorway, she paused and peered around it before entering, taking in the sight of her mother sitting at the table with her laptop open in front of her and papers strewn all about. Before Raven could say anything or step farther into the room, her mom glanced up and caught sight of her.

"Hey, Mom." She pushed herself off the wall and stepped fully into the room.

"Raven." Her mom's hands fell away from the computer keys, and she slowly closed the laptop.

Raven shifted uneasily under the unwavering gaze. "Where's Dad?"

"Hockey game with your uncle Frank."

"What are you doing?"

"Just some paperwork. Come sit." She nodded toward the chair across from hers. After a moment's hesitation, Raven shuffled across the kitchen and slid into the seat.

"I want to apologize for last night," her mom began. "You're father and I, we didn't handle the news as well as we could have."

Raven nodded. She wasn't going to argue with that. Nor was she going to say it was all right, because it wasn't.

"It's going to take me some time to get used to the idea," her mom continued. "But I'll get there."

She noticed her mother said I, not we. "And Dad?"

"Your father is struggling," her mom said softly. "And I realize that isn't fair to you, but you're going to have to be patient with him. Eventually, he'll come around."

Raven had been hearing that a lot lately, and frankly, she was getting tired of it. She didn't understand why she was the one who had to be patient, be understanding, and wait for everyone else to come around to realizing she was still the same person she'd always been.

"His father, your grandfather, was a very hard man. Very rigid."

Raven nodded to show she was following, even though she didn't really see where this was going.

"He was also very bigoted. He had prejudices against pretty much everyone. Your father is a very different type of man, but there are some things that, right or wrong, each of us believes because it's what we're taught when we're young."

Abstractly, she understood that, but it didn't make her own father rejecting her any easier.

"So now your dad's struggling against his upbringing. Trying to reconcile the things his father taught him with things he's facing now."

Raven didn't really know what to say. It wasn't as if any of this was her mom's fault, so taking her anger and frustration out on her wouldn't really accomplish anything.

"He'll come around," her mom repeated.

It was probably meant to be comforting.

It wasn't.

"Your father said he wouldn't be home until late," her mom said after a beat of silence. "We're on our own for supper. Want to get some Indian food and watch a movie? Talk a little?"

It sounded like it would be so incredibly awkward to sit and talk to her mother about this, but Raven wanted things to go back to normal: just another night when her dad was out and she and her mom ordered food he didn't like and watched movies he didn't care for.

"Sounds good," she said. "Want me to order while you finish up?"

"That'd be great, hon. Thanks."

CHAPTER THIRTY-TWO

Raven had just finished setting up in the living room, paper plates, cups, and napkins arranged across the coffee table, turning it into a makeshift dining room, when the doorbell rang. A few minutes later, her mom strode into the room, laden down with takeout bags.

"How many people were you planning on feeding?" Mom asked, nodding toward the assortment of containers she was laying out on the coffee table.

"Hey, you're the one who always wants seconds."

Her mother just shook her head as she settled on the couch.

A comfortable silence settled as they served themselves, but it grew awkward as they sat back with their plates full, no longer distracted by the act of carefully arranging the various offerings.

"So, what are we watching?" Raven asked, hating the way her voice wavered in the air between them.

Mom shrugged and nodded to the remote on the coffee table, half buried beneath takeout containers. "Whatever you'd like."

Carefully balancing her plate in one hand, she leaned forward and snagged the remote. The TV turned on with a click that rang out like a shot in the otherwise silent room.

After a quick perusal of the movie channel's offerings, Raven didn't see anything that interested her, but she couldn't bear the thought of the awkward conversation and the equally awkward intermittent silences, so she clicked on the most recent addition to the lineup, barely even reading the title.

Despite being hungry a moment ago, her food looked unappealing now. She took a couple of bites that were tasteless on her tongue and settled heavily in her stomach. Her eyes were on the screen in front of her, but she barely saw what was going on as she sat there, tense and waiting for her mother to say something.

They made it through the opening credits and about ten minutes of the movie before her mother shifted beside her and took a deep breath: a clear sign that she was working her way up to speaking. It gave Raven just enough time to take a deep, calming breath of her own.

"Now that you're dating someone seriously, this Morgan—" She stumbled slightly over the name, and Raven tried not to react, but she was pretty sure her mother saw her flinch. "I think it would be appropriate to set up some ground rules."

It was clear the conversation, her own words, were making her mother uncomfortable, but she kept going.

Raven had to give her credit for that, even if she didn't want to talk about Morgan anymore right now. Not to mention that it didn't really matter anyway. They weren't together anymore. "Mom—"

"I don't really feel comfortable with you spending so much time with someone I haven't met."

Raven's protest died on her lips at her mother's words. That wasn't what she'd been expecting at all. She'd thought her mother was going to ban her from driving out there on weeknights, or renegotiate her curfew, or in some other way attempt to keep them from spending much time together.

"I think…" She faltered, then pressed on "I think you should invite her over for dinner. Next weekend."

Clearly, the invitation was an effort for her mother, but all that mattered was she'd made the offer.

"Mom, that's…I…" She wanted to express how much the invitation meant to her, but the words got caught in her throat. After a moment, she shook her head. "Morgan and I broke up," she admitted.

Her mother turned, looking at her full on for the first time since this conversation had started with eyes wide and full of surprise. "What? When did this happen?"

"Last night." She felt the sting of tears against her lids, but she blinked them off. As painful as it was to think about Morgan, let alone talk about her, she wanted to tell her mother. Up until a moment ago, she hadn't believed that her mother would be willing to even try to understand how much she was hurting right now. But the dinner invitation changed things. Raven wanted to know just how supportive her mother really was.

Haltingly, she began to explain the fight to her mother, and soon everything was just rushing out, the words tumbling out of her mouth so quickly that her mom kept stopping her to remind her to breathe.

By the time she was finished, Raven was breathless and crying openly, the tears coursing down her cheeks. She brought her gaze up to meet her mother's, on edge as she waited to hear what she would say.

Her mom didn't say a word. She simply reached out and pulled Raven into a hug, wrapping her arms around her and holding her tightly.

CHAPTER THIRTY-THREE

Raven could hear the faint murmur of conversation and the clattering of dishes from downstairs when she woke, so she went through her morning routine slowly, half hoping that by the time she finished, her parents would have left for work, even as she felt a growing need to see where things stood with her father. When she couldn't avoid facing him any longer, when not only her nerves, but her stomach urged her to go downstairs, she took a deep, fortifying breath, grabbed her backpack, and left the safety of her room.

She reached the bottom of the staircase and rounded the corner, almost running smack into her father. They both pulled up short and stared at each other.

"Hey, Dad." She dropped her eyes and stepped back.

"Raven." He gave her a curt nod and eased around her. She trailed him into the kitchen but paused just inside the doorway as he crossed the room to the stove.

"Morning, honey," her mom said, glancing up from whatever she was mixing at the counter. "Are you having breakfast with us? Your father's making pancakes."

It was perhaps the only thing he could make—a fact they'd teased him about endlessly over the years. She had a feeling there would be no such banter this morning. She glanced over at her dad. He had his back to her as he adjusted dials on the stove and poked at the bacon she could see starting to sizzle.

"Yeah, sure," she said to her mom finally, holding in a sigh. Her mom beamed at her, and Raven couldn't help but smile back.

"Do you want blueberries in yours?" Her father's question drew her attention toward him. "I think we still have some in the freezer." He didn't look at her as he spoke, and his voice was flat, lacking warmth or inflection, but she knew the question was directed toward her, because her mom was allergic to blueberries.

She stared at the back of his head for a long moment, then cleared her throat. "Yeah." She winced at the slight rasp in her response. "Blueberries would be good."

He nodded but didn't reply as he turned toward the fridge. Raven watched him for a moment, then turned her attention back to her mother, whose smile had turned sad. Raven shrugged and averted her gaze.

"Can I help with anything?" she asked, if only to break the tension in the room.

Her mom shook her head. "No. Just sit. Talk to me."

It could have been a typical weekday morning, if not for the fact that her father hovered just outside the periphery of her vision, stubbornly silent as he stacked pancakes onto the serving platter at his elbow. His lack of participation in the conversation was glaring. Or at least it was to Raven.

Even when he came to the table with his stack of golden brown pancakes and just the right combination of crispy and soft bacon, he remained silent. Instead of chiming in with stories about his students, he ate slowly and methodically. Raven couldn't tell if he was even listening to their conversation; his face remained impassive.

She wondered if this was how it was going to be from now on, awkward silences and heavy tension, her dad only speaking to her when it was unavoidable, and her mom sending her sad, sympathetic glances.

"Dad?"

He stopped eating at the sound of her voice, and for the first time all morning, turned to look at her.

"I don't like it, and I can't say I understand it. But I'm not going to stop you," he said, answering the question she had not yet asked. His voice wasn't harsh or angry, but rather quiet, matter of fact. Raven wasn't sure whether that was better or worse.

"I swore if I ever had kids I wouldn't be like my father," he continued. "That I wouldn't try to control my children, or dictate their lives."

Raven nodded, even though he wasn't actually looking at her.

"Like I said, I don't like it. But I won't stop you."

It was what Raven had been expecting, but it still stung just the same.

"I'm going to be late for school," she murmured, pushing her chair back roughly and springing to her feet. Her mom reached out, laying a hand on her arm, but she shrugged it off and headed for the front door.

Tears blurred her vision, and she knew she was in no shape to drive.

If she hurried, she could make it to Summer's in time for a ride. She was out the door before she'd even finished putting on her boots. She stutter-stepped across the porch, pulling her boots on hastily and then slung her other arm through her coat, as she started down the walkway.

Summer's car still sat in her driveway when Raven arrived, so she went around to the side door and let herself in. The kitchen stood empty, Summer's parents having already left for the day. She headed upstairs. Summer's door was open, so she didn't bother knocking, just stepped into the room, and then paused when two sets of eyes turned to her.

"Summer. Chloe."

From the way they both fell silent she knew they'd been talking about her.

"Hey, Raven." Summer gave her a warm, albeit slightly awkward smile, while Chloe simply nodded her head in greeting.

The day wasn't starting off so hot. She was tempted to turn around and go home, hide in her room all day. If her father wasn't gone yet, he would be soon. The thing was, she didn't really want to be alone with her thoughts. She was looking forward to the distraction of school—or at least she had been. She didn't know if she'd be able to face it if her friends were going to act weird all day.

After a moment's hesitation in the doorway, she decided to plow through, pretend everything was normal. Maybe if she did, eventually, it would be. "Can I bum a ride?" she asked as she crossed the room and flopped down on the bed. She landed next to Chloe, jostling her and brushing against her leg. Beside her, she felt Chloe stiffen, and then slowly inch her calf away from Raven's shoulder. She tried to pretend she didn't notice, but it stung.

"Sure thing," Summer's answer was mostly lost amongst the buzzing in her head, but she managed to mumble a quick thanks, before staring at the ceiling and trying to find patterns in the spackle, as a heavy silence fell over the room.

"So…you guys ready to go?"

Raven nodded and rolled off the bed. A moment later, Chloe followed suit, still keeping a careful distance from Raven as the three of them made their way downstairs in silence. She was glad it was a short drive to school.

Ten minutes of awkward silence, punctuated by overly cheerful radio jockeys later, they were climbing out of Summer's car and heading in different directions. Or rather, Chloe was heading off on her own to meet AJ before classes started.

Raven hated feeling happy to see Chloe go.

"Hey." Summer's hand on her elbow pulled her out of her thoughts, and Raven turned her head to face her. "She'll come around."

❖

School was a waste, for the amount of attention she paid to her morning classes. She tried to take notes and follow along, but her concentration was shot. By the time lunch rolled around, Raven had decided to ditch the rest of the day and go home. When the bell rang releasing them from classes, Raven headed for her locker instead of the cafeteria, only to be caught up short when she spotted Summer leaning against her locker waiting for her.

"Hey," she called out as she approached. "What's up?"

Summer should be in the cafeteria securing them a decent table. Her class was the closest, so it generally fell to her to make sure they didn't get stuck sitting in the back by the recycling and garbage bins or under the draft of the windows.

"Just thought I'd walk you to lunch." Summer's tone was too casual, her smile a little too bright. She had definitely guessed that Raven was going to take off. Raven just couldn't figure out why she was trying to stop her. She opened her mouth to protest, but before she could speak up, Summer continued, "Avoiding her isn't going to fix your friendship."

"I'm not the one avoiding *her*."

"The only way you two are going to get past this is if you spend some time together. Show her that you're still the same person she's known for the last ten years."

As much as she hated to admit it, Raven knew Summer was right. The only way to get through to Chloe was to show her that nothing had changed. But she just wasn't up for it today. She started to beg off, but caught Summer's hopeful gaze, the pleading in her eyes, and sighed. "Fine, lead the way. But as soon as lunch is over, I'm gone."

CHAPTER THIRTY-FOUR

I'm so sick of this day," Raven said by way of greeting, as she strode through Summer's open bedroom door. "Can I stay here tonight?" she asked, as she dropped her backpack onto the floor and flopped onto her bed. "I really don't want to be at home right now."

She had spent the afternoon wallowing around the house, rereading all the texts she and Morgan had exchanged, because, despite the ache they created in her chest, she simply could not get enough. She couldn't bear to be there when her parents got home though. She just wasn't up to facing her dad.

"Of course you can stay here," Summer said. "But Chloe and I are working on a project for sociology."

Raven's head shot up at the mention of Chloe's name and offered a weak smile when she spotted her leaning against the side of Summer's desk.

"If you want to hang for a bit we can do a movie or something when we're done," Summer continued. "Make a girls' night out of it."

Raven hesitated. Trading in the awkwardness at home for awkwardness with Chloe wasn't really what she'd had in mind for the evening. "Sounds good," she said finally. Summer nodded and then turned an appraising eye on Chloe, who looked about as uncomfortable as Raven felt. After a moment under her expectant stare, she nodded.

"Awesome," Summer said with a grin. "It shouldn't take us more than an hour to finish up here. If you want to watch something…" She tossed the remote over. Raven caught it and then placed it on the bedside table in favor of pulling out her phone.

"What's wrong with being at home?" Chloe asked. It was the first thing she'd said to Raven all day, but Raven wasn't in the mood to get into it with her. She shrugged.

"Raven's dad hasn't spoken to her since she came out," Summer said when Raven remained silent.

"Oh, Rae, that sucks," Chloe said.

When Raven chanced a glance over at her, she looked genuinely upset. She didn't have the energy to point out the irony of her comment. Instead, she turned her attention back to her texts and tried to ignore the prickly feeling along the back of her neck that told her she was being stared at.

"So what do you say we finish this up tomorrow and start that movie now?" Summer suggested, way too brightly.

"As long as it's not one of those horror flicks you guys love so much," Chloe said. "I'd like to actually be able to sleep tonight."

Raven and Summer exchanged glances. Seeing the look, Chloe let out a sigh. "Fine. But I'm sleeping here. And the light stays on."

❖

"Worst. Movie. Ever," Chloe said as soon as the screen faded to black and the credits started rolling up the screen.

"How would you know? You barely watched any of it," Summer countered.

Chloe opened her mouth to reply, but Raven interrupted their banter as she pushed herself to her feet.

"I'm going to make some popcorn," she said as she started for the kitchen, not sure if either of them heard her, or if they were even paying attention.

"Make two bags," Summer called out after her. "Oh. And can you bring me a drink?"

"Sure thing."

"And there are chips in the cupboard. Would you get them too?"

"Is that all?" Raven teased as she spun around in the doorway. "Or would you like anything else?"

Summer pretended to consider for a minute. "Nope. That'll be all. Unless you're really hungry, then there's a pizza in the freezer."

Raven rolled her eyes but nodded.

"I'll help," Chloe said softly and pushed herself to her feet and followed Raven into the kitchen.

The silence between them was heavy, expectant, as they moved around the kitchen and each other with practiced familiarity. Within minutes, they had everything set up; the pizza was heating in the oven, the popcorn was turning in the microwave, the glasses were full of ice and soda, and the bowls were stacked next to the bag of chips.

With nothing left to distract them, the tension grew. Raven leaned against the counter and absently read the magnets and comic strips on the fridge, while Chloe fidgeted in a chair at the table across from her. Finally, she cleared her throat.

Raven stiffened, waiting.

"I know I've been pretty crappy in the friend department lately," Chloe said softly. "I'm sorry. It just took me a couple of days to wrap my head around it."

Raven nodded once.

"I didn't feel like I knew you anymore. I didn't—I don't—really know how to talk to you."

"I'm the same person I've been all along, Chlo."

"Really? It doesn't feel like it," Chloe said softly. "We used to tell each other everything. And then I find out you have this whole other side to you that I had absolutely no idea about."

"It's not like I was keeping secrets to hurt you. I was afraid—terrified—of how you'd react if I told you. And guess what? It was a valid concern," Raven added. "Because when I told you, you couldn't deal."

"I know. That's why I'm apologizing. You're my best friend and I don't want to lose you. I'm trying, okay?"

"You shouldn't have to try," Raven snapped. "If you're my best friend I should be able to tell you anything and have you accept it. Accept me."

"I know. It's just a lot to take in. And you didn't exactly make it easy for me. You told me, and then you shut down. I didn't feel like I could talk to you about it."

"Well, I'm sorry my personal crisis has been so hard on you."

"See, this is what I'm talking about. I'm trying to talk to you and you're not hearing me. I don't know how to deal with you anymore."

"I haven't changed, Chloe. If you can't deal, that's on you."

"I'm trying to fix things. You're shutting me down."

Chloe's words gave her pause. Was she being unfairly harsh to her? Chloe's behavior over the past week had hurt, but she was here now and she seemed sincere in her efforts. And, wait. Wasn't that all she had wanted, for Chloe to be back in her life? She didn't like the awkward tension that hung between them. She wanted things to normal again. But…if she just gave in, wasn't that like saying the way Chloe had treated her was okay?

"I know I've got a lot of making up to do," Chloe said, "but it won't work if you don't let me."

Raven slumped against the counter, all the fight draining out of her. "Okay."

A hesitant smile tugged at the corners of Chloe's lips.

"I wanted to tell you," Raven said softly into the silence, thinking back to all the nights she caught herself, phone in hand, about to call one of her friends. She'd gone through so much in the last few weeks, confusion and uncertainty, excitement and happiness, and she'd gone through most of it alone.

"You can tell me now," Chloe said, equally soft. "You can tell me about her. What happened between you two anyway?"

Raven blinked at the question, feeling that familiar lump at the base of her throat as her mind flashed back to their last conversation. "She needed more than I was ready to give."

"More as in…" Chloe's eyebrow arched in question, and Raven blushed as she realized what her explanation could have been alluding to.

"No. No, we weren't anywhere ready for that." Raven swallowed back her nervousness. "She wanted someone who could hold her hand in public and wasn't uncomfortable with people knowing they were together. She had an art show she wanted me to go to. And I just couldn't. We got into a fight about it on Saturday."

"Are you guys broken up? Or are you just in a fight?"

"Is there a difference?"

"Well, yeah," Chloe said, the "duh" heavily implied. "Couples fight all the time. But it doesn't always mean they're broken up."

"How do you know which one it is?" she asked slowly, because it had felt pretty final to her. But if there was even a chance...

She held her breath, waiting for Chloe's answer.

"Depends on what the fight was about. Whether or not the thing that caused it can be changed. Fixed."

Raven tried not to read too much into Chloe's words, tried not to let the faint stirring of hope in her chest grow, until she was sure what Chloe was implying. "This fight you and Morgan had, about you not being able to be there for her, publicly. Has that changed? Could you go to this art show thing and hold her hand? Be her girlfriend?"

Raven considered it. She'd come out to her family, to her friends. She and Morgan wouldn't have to lie or sneak around. While being out and open about their relationship was still a frightening prospect, the pull of fear wasn't nearly as strong as the remembered warmth of Morgan's hand in hers, and the pleasant flutter of butterflies she got when Morgan smiled at her.

She glanced over at Chloe, and saw she was fidgeting in her chair, staring at her expectantly.

"Yeah. I could," she said, smiling even as tears pooled in her eyes.

Chapter Thirty-five

R aven paused just outside the door of the art gallery, trying to calm her racing heart. She clutched the bouquet of flowers tightly in both hands in an attempt to stop them from shaking. After a moment, Raven exhaled slowly and pushed through the door. Once inside, she paused once again, this time letting her gaze roam around the room, trying to take it all in but it was all just a blur of faces and colors. She blinked and forced herself to focus, scanning the room until she found what she was looking for. Or who.

Morgan.

She stood on the other side of the room, head bent in conversation with another girl. Raven took in the sight of them standing close, Morgan's hand resting on Cindy's elbow, and her blood ran cold. It had never occurred to her that Morgan might have moved on already, that she might have brought a date. Then the girl's head tipped back in laughter, and Raven realized it was Cindy. She let out a sigh of relief and sagged momentarily against the door behind her.

Cindy glanced up as she approached and offered a small smile, but Morgan didn't seem to register her presence until Raven came to a stop directly in front of her. Morgan's gaze drifted up, and she blinked owlishly.

"What are you doing here?" Morgan's tone wasn't exactly accusatory, but it wasn't welcoming either. It didn't escape Raven's notice the way Morgan's grip tightened on Cindy's arm for support.

Raven's words died in the back of her throat. The carefully crafted speech that she, Summer, and Chloe had spent hours working on last night vanished from her brain. She stood there feeling awkward and tongue-tied, death-gripping the bouquet of flowers until the stems dug painfully into her palms. Instead of answering the question directly, Raven lifted the bouquet into Morgan's eye line and pressed it gently into her hands. "I got you these."

Morgan's fingers closed around the stems automatically. "That's sweet of you," she said. "But you shouldn't have."

Raven searched her mind for what she'd meant to say. For the eloquence she'd practiced last night, but her thoughts were a jumble inside her head. "I miss you," she said. "I miss you, and I want to get back together," she added, then bit back a groan at how ungraceful she was being.

"Oh, Raven." Morgan's tone was gentle, sympathetic, but also cautious, and Raven couldn't help but recoil slightly from it. Morgan was seconds away from letting her down easy, and she couldn't let that happen.

"I came out to my parents," she blurted, wincing at how her words ran together in her rush to get them out. "To my friends. I'm out now."

"That's...I don't know what to say. I'm proud of you. For coming out."

Raven nodded and allowed herself a moment to soak up the warmth of Morgan's words, and her gentle smile before shaking her head, dispelling the feeling. That wasn't why she was here. "I'm sorry I hurt you. Sorry I made you feel like I was ashamed of being with you. Because I wasn't. Not once. I was proud to be with you. I was just afraid." She took a step closer and felt a stirring of hope when Morgan didn't immediately take a step back.

"But I'm not afraid anymore. My mom wants you to come to dinner some night. And yeah, it'll have to be on a night when my dad's not around, but the point is, I want you to meet her. I want to introduce you to my friends as my girlfriend and take you out and hold your hand, because I don't care if anyone sees us." She met Morgan's gaze with pleading eyes. She needed Morgan to see that she was being serious about this, that she was ready for this, for them. "Just give me another chance. Please?" She reached out and took Morgan's hand, lacing their fingers together and giving a gentle squeeze. She stared searchingly into Morgan's eyes.

A grin tugged at the corners of Morgan's lips. "Okay."

It was more of a sigh than a word, a breathless exhalation so quiet that Raven almost missed it. At the last moment, she realized what Morgan had said. "Yeah?" She smiled so wide that it hurt but she couldn't stop.

Morgan nodded. "Yeah."

Raven's free hand came up and cupped Morgan's face, the pads of her fingers sliding gently across her smooth skin, as she dipped her head and, heedless of the crowd around them, captured Morgan's lips with her own. Morgan smiled into the kiss and wrapped her arms around Raven's waist, pulling her close. Raven went willingly, openly, knowing she was finally exactly where she should be and exactly who she should be: herself. Nothing more, and—never again—nothing less.

About the Author

Growing up in a small town in Southern Ontario, Samantha Hale was an avid reader who fell in love with the written word in all its forms. She was fascinated with the way a book could take her away to another world and began writing, finding that she loved creating her own worlds just as much as she loved reading about the ones in her favorite novels.

Soliloquy Titles From Bold Strokes Books

Searching for Grace by Juliann Rich. First it's a rumor. Then it's a fact. And then it's on. (978-1-62639-196-3)

Dark Tide by Greg Herren. A summer working as a lifeguard at a hotel on the Gulf Coast seems like a dream job...until Ricky Hackworth realizes the town is shielding some very dark—and deadly—secrets. (978-1-62639-197-0)

Everything Changes by Samantha Hale. Raven Walker's world is turned upside down the moment Morgan O'Shea walks into her life. (978-1-62639-303-5)

Tristant and Elijah by Jennifer Lavoie. After Elijah finds a scandalous letter belonging to Tristant's great uncle, the boys set out to discover the secret Uncle Glenn kept hidden his entire life and end up discovering who they are in the process. (978-1-62639-075-1)

Caught in the Crossfire by Juliann Rich. Two boys at Bible camp; one forbidden love. (978-1-62639-070-6)

Remember Me by Melanie Batchelor. After a tragic event occurs, teenager Jamie Richards is left questioning the identity of the girl she loved, Erica Sinclair. (978-1-62639-184-0)

Frenemy of the People by Nora Olsen. Clarissa and Lexie have despised each other as long as they can remember, but when they both find themselves helping an unlikely contender for homecoming queen, they are catapulted into an unexpected romance. (978-1-62639-063-8)

The Balance by Neal Wooten. Love and survival come together in the distant future as Piri and Niko faceoff against the worst factions of mankind's evolution. (978-1-62639-055-3)

The Unwanted by Jeffrey Ricker. Jamie Thomas is plunged into danger when he discovers his mother is an Amazon who needs his help to save the tribe from a vengeful god. (978-1-62639-048-5)

Because of Her by KE Payne. When Tabby Morton is forced to move to London, she's convinced her life will never be the same again. But the beautiful and intriguing Eden Palmer is about to show her that this time, change is most definitely for the better. (978-1-62639-049-2)

Asher's Fault by Elizabeth Wheeler. Fourteen-year-old Asher Price sees the world in black and white, much like the photos he takes, but when his little brother drowns at the same moment Asher experiences his first same-sex kiss, he can no longer hide behind the lens of his camera and eventually discovers he isn't the only one with a secret. (978-1-60282-982-4)

The Seventh Pleiade by Andrew J. Peters. When Atlantis is besieged by violent storms, tremors, and a barbarian army, it will be up to a young gay prince to find a way for the kingdom's survival. (978-1-60282-960-2)

The Missing Juliet: A Fisher Key Adventure by Sam Cameron. A teenage detective and her friends search for a kidnapped Hollywood star in the Florida Keys. (978-1-60282-959-6)

Meeting Chance by Jennifer Lavoie. When man's best friend turns on Aaron Cassidy, the teen keeps his distance until fate puts Chance in his hands. (978-1-60282-952-7)

Lake Thirteen by Greg Herren. A visit to an old cemetery seems like fun to a group of five teenagers, who soon learn that sometimes it's best to leave old ghosts alone. (978-1-60282-894-0)

The Road to Her by KE Payne. Sparks fly when actress Holly Croft, star of UK soap *Portobello Road*, meets her new on-screen love interest, the enigmatic and sexy Elise Manford. (978-1-60282-887-2)

Swans and Klons by Nora Olsen. In a future world where there are no males, sixteen-year-old Rubric and her girlfriend Salmon Jo must fight to survive when everything they believed in turns out to be a lie. (978-1-60282-874-2)

Kings of Ruin by Sam Cameron. High school student Danny Kelly and loner Kevin Clark must team up to defeat a top-secret alien intelligence that likes to wreak havoc with fiery car, truck, and train accidents. (978-1-60282-864-3)

Wonderland by David-Matthew Barnes. After her mother's sudden death, Destiny Moore is sent to live with her two gay uncles on Avalon Cove, a mysterious island on which she uncovers a secret place called Wonderland, where love and magic prove to be real. (978-1-60282-788-2)

Another 365 Days by KE Payne. Clemmie Atkins is back, and her life is more complicated than ever! Still madly in love with her girlfriend, Clemmie suddenly finds her life turned upside down with distractions, confessions, and the return of a familiar face… (978-1-60282-775-2)

The Secret of Othello by Sam Cameron. Florida teen detectives Steven and Denny risk their lives to search for a sunken NASA satellite—but under the waves, no one can hear you scream… (978-1-60282-742-4)

Andy Squared by Jennifer Lavoie. Andrew never thought anyone could come between him and his twin sister, Andrea… until Ryder rode into town. (978-1-60282-743-1)

Sara by Greg Herren. A mysterious and beautiful new student at Southern Heights High School stirs things up when students start dying. (978-1-60282-674-8)

OMGqueer edited by Radclyffe and Katherine E. Lynch, PhD. Through stories imagined and told by youth across America, this anthology provides a snapshot of queerness at the dawn of the new millennium. (978-1-60282-682-3)

Street Dreams by Tama Wise. Tyson Rua has more than his fair share of problems growing up in New Zealand—he's gay, he's falling in love, and he's run afoul of the local hip-hop crew leader just as he's trying to make it as a graffiti artist. (978-1-60282-650-2)

me@you.com by KE Payne. Is it possible to fall in love with someone you've never met? Imogen Summers thinks so because it's happened to her. (978-1-60282-592-5)

Swimming to Chicago by David-Matthew Barnes. As the lives of the adults around them unravel, high school students Alex and Robby form an unbreakable bond, vowing to do anything to stay together—even if it means leaving everything behind. (978-1-60282-572-7)

365 Days by KE Payne. Life sucks when you're seventeen years old and confused about your sexuality, and the girl of your dreams doesn't even know you exist. Then in walks sexy new emo girl, Hannah Harrison. Clemmie Atkins has exactly 365 days to discover herself, and she's going to have a blast doing it! (978-1-60282-540-6)

Timothy by Greg Herren. *Timothy* is a romantic suspense thriller from award-winning mystery writer Greg Herren set in the fabulous Hamptons. (978-1-60282-760-8)